Nana's Naughty Knickers

by Katherine DiSavino

A SAMUEL FRENCH ACTING EDITION

SAMUEL FRENCH

FOUNDED 1830

NEW YORK HOLLYWOOD LONDON TORONTO

SAMUELFRENCH.COM

ISBN 978-0-573-69793-7   Printed in U.S.A.   #29291

MUSIC USE NOTE

IMPORTANT BILLING AND CREDIT REQUIREMENTS

NANA'S NAUGHTY KNICKERS was first produced by the Rainbow Dinner Theatre in Paradise, Pennsylvania on February 5, 2010. The play was produced by David DiSavino and Cynthia DiSavino, with direction, set, and costume design by Cynthia DiSavino and sound design by David DiSavino. The production stage manager was Scott Russell. The cast was as follows:

SYLVIA CHARLES	Sherry Konjura
VERA WALTERS	Lois Sharrot
BRIDGET CHARLES	Sarah Buck
TOM O'GRADY	Craig A. Smith
MR. SCHMIDT	Joe Winters
HEATHER VAN PREE	Maria Jones
CLAIR	Casey Allyn
VOICE	Scott Russell
UPS MAN	Robbie Ringer
OTHER UPS MAN	John Delancey

CHARACTERS

SYLVIA CHARLES – In her early eighties, living like she's in her early twenties. The mastermind behind Saucy Slips, Etc., and the proud tenant of a rent controlled apartment.

VERA WALTERS – Sylvia's aged accomplice: equipped with two hearing aids and a collapsible walker.

BRIDGET CHARLES – Sylvia's unsuspecting, 20-something, soon-to-be-law-student granddaughter.

TOM O'GRADY – The newest cop on the force, happily assigned the beat where Sylvia's apartment is.

GIL SCHMIDT – The landlord, overly eager to rid himself of his aged tenants. 60s.

HEATHER VAN PREE – Employee of Saucy Lips, looking for better opportunities, a modeling career, or just her boxes.

CLAIR – The big client. Mid 60s.

VOICE – The man at the front desk. Slightly bored and always sarcastic. Can double as one of the UPS men.

UPS MAN – Cute and a little lonely.

OTHER UPS MAN – The strong and silent type. For doubling purposes, this could be the same actor that plays Heather, Clair or Mr. Schmidt, as long as the audience doesn't recognize them as such.

A NOTE ON THE SET

I realize that not every theatre will have the capabilities to create a set which functions the exact way that is described in the script. If you can't do it the way that it's written, that does not mean you can't do this play! Instead, use what I've written in the set descriptions as a guideline and find ways that work for your space to do the big reveals. A production of *Nana's Naughty Knickers* took place in North Carolina at a theatre entirely in the round, which meant that there wasn't a physical "set" at all – no doors or walls. So instead of the walls of the set functioning as the hiding places for Sylvia's collection of lingerie, physical set pieces had to serve this purpose instead.

The point is, have fun with whatever set you choose to build for your production. I wish you all the best of luck.

-Katherine DiSavino

ACT ONE

(Lights up on a well-decorated, albeit cluttered, apartment on the Upper East Side of New York City. A large comfortable couch is the prominent feature of the living room: worn and welcoming with throw pillows of a decidedly more modern mode.

There is a hallway that leads to an unseen part of the apartment where the study and guest room are located; on the opposite side of the stage is the front door. On the upstage side of the front door is a simple coat rack with wooden pegs attached to the wall. It has a shelf over the top of the pegs, enclosed by a decorative captain's rail. Further upstage from the pegboard is a large bookshelf.

A fireplace is opposite the front door.

There is also a bedroom door, a kitchen door, a bathroom door and a closet door. The closet door must be placed on a wall where the interior of the closet can be seen.

BRIDGET *and* **TOM** *enter through the front door.* **BRIDGET** *has a rolling suitcase, a large bag and a box in her arms.* **TOM**, *in his NYPD uniform, is struggling to balance two large boxes and one medium sized one – clearly straining under their weight – and valiantly trying to hide it.)*

BRIDGET. Nana? Hey Nana? *(crosses to the downstage left side of the couch.)(To* **TOM***)* Thank you so much for helping me with these boxes!

TOM. Well, I figured I should help unload before I give you a ticket for double-parking.

BRIDGET. Right! Ticket! *(pause)* What?

TOM. Just some law enforcement humor. *(laughs nervously, hovering by the door, a stack of heavy boxes in his arms)* You should move your car, though…It's blocking the street.

BRIDGET. Of course! No, you're right – I'll move it right away. I really appreciate all your help. I know you're "on duty" and everything…

TOM. My pleasure, Bridge – I was keeping an eye out for when you'd come…

BRIDGET. Really? Wow, Tom, that's so –

TOM. Um, Bridget?

BRIDGET. Yes?

TOM. These boxes are really heavy – Can I – ?

BRIDGET. Oh! Sure! Sorry. Just put them here. You okay?

TOM. I'm fine Bridge. No worries! *(pause)* Do you know a chiropractor?

BRIDGET. *(Laughing. Stops.)* Wait, are you serious? Oh! Sit down. D'you want advil? A heat pack? Some –

TOM. No, no, it's okay. I'm just kidding – sort of. Hey, how long did you say you were going to be staying here?

BRIDGET. Just for the summer. I want to have my own place by the time I start classes –

TOM. Law school, right?

BRIDGET. Yeah. How did you –?

TOM. Sylvia told me. She's pretty excited you're moving in – even if it's only temporary.

BRIDGET. Since when did you get on a first name basis with my 83 year-old Nana, Tom?

TOM. Ever since I programmed the speed dials into her cell phone three months ago.

BRIDGET. You're the culprit! She's been calling me non-stop!

TOM. Yeah, I know. I put you as number two.

BRIDGET. Who's number one?

TOM. Me.

BRIDGET. You're the local law!

> (**BRIDGET** *and* **TOM** *sit on the couch together –
> but not "together" – a slightly awkward, very sweet
> duo.*)

TOM. Well, now she can call if she needs help and I
can come right up. A lady her age – I don't like to
think about her all by herself.

BRIDGET. *(scoots closer to him on the couch)* Well, it's really
sweet of you. It means a lot to me – her having
someone like you around, I mean.

TOM. Yeah? I hoped it would. Mean a lot to you, that is.

BRIDGET. Really?

TOM. Yeah. *(Closes the gap between them. Faintly romantic.)*
Bridget, can I ask you something?

BRIDGET. *(big breath)* Anything.

TOM. Well – *(He reaches towards her cheek.)* Sometimes…
does she *(He kind of rubs at her face a little.)* You
know…Does she always find dirt on your face?

BRIDGET. *(crestfallen)* Huh?

TOM. I've been wondering for a while if it's just me.
You know, like I walk around with smudges on my
nose all the time and never realize it –

BRIDGET. What?

TOM. You know – with the –

> *(He licks his thumb and tries to demonstrate by rub-
> bing something off of* **BRIDGET**'s *face again.)*

The dirt-rub!

BRIDGET. *(She swats his hand away.)* Yes, yes, yes – okay!
–She does that to everyone. You're lucky she only
points out the dirt to you – for me, it's the zits.

TOM. You wouldn't think a lady her age would have
eyesight that sharp.

BRIDGET. No, her eyesight is fine - her taste I'm starting to question. Look at these pillows. When did she get these?.

TOM. A few weeks ago. Said she was going for a different "feel" in here.

BRIDGET. Yeah. I guess you could call it that.

TOM. It's cute! She's just trying to bring a younger vibe to the place since you're here now, I bet. Hey, is it okay if I wash up in the bathroom before I head out?

BRIDGET. Yeah, sure!

(**TOM** *exits into the bathroom. As soon as the bathroom door snaps shut,* **SYLVIA** *– 80 years young – bounds through the front door of the apartment in a sweat suit with matching sweat bands on her forehead and wrists, and a folded up walker held above her, like a trophy.*)

SYLVIA. Made it all the way down to 49th and back in forty-five minutes and I didn't even break a sweat! Or a hip! *(seeing* **BRIDGET***)* Hello Pumpkin Face!

(*She hugs* **BRIDGET***, pulls back and holds her at arms length, inspecting her.*)

Oh. Bridget! You have one heck of a pimple on your chin. Let's pop it!

(**SYLVIA** *lunges at* **BRIDGET***, eager to pop the offending pimple.* **BRIDGET** *dances out of the way.*)

BRIDGET. Whoa, Nana! I'll get it later – Hey, I didn't know you had a walker.

SYLVIA. This? Oh no, sugar, this isn't mine. I took it from Vera – we're doing a new kind of therapy together.

BRIDGET. Physical therapy?

SYLVIA. No, motivational therapy. She wants her walker back, so she's motivated to chase me down Fifth Avenue to get it.

(**SYLVIA** *walks to the open front door and yells into the stairwell –*)

VERA, let's get a move-on! They'll have my headstone carved by the time you make it up here!

VERA. *(off)* I don't know what the hell you're shouting, but I'm waiting for the elevator.

(**SLYVIA** *rolls her eyes and crosses to the bathroom.*)

BRIDGET. Oh, no, Nana. Tom – I mean *Officer* O'Grady's in there. He helped me carry some of my things up.

SYLVIA. Tom's here? Such a good little police officer… Bridget, have you noticed what a wonderful little officer Tom is?

BRIDGET. Nana.

SYLVIA. And single, too. He's single, Bridget.

BRIDGET. *Nana.*

SYLVIA. You know, I was just telling him the other day about how you couldn't stop talking about him after you two met a few months ago!

BRIDGET. Nana!

VERA. *(stands in doorway, clinging to the frame)* My God, Sylvia, give me that walker so I can beat you over the head with it!

BRIDGET. Hi Vera!

VERA. Hey, kid. Don't mind me while I lay down in the doorway and die.

SYLVIA. Stop being so dramatic. You almost caught up to me outside of Saks Fifth Avenue.

VERA. That was only because you stopped to look at the lingerie display!

SYLVIA. I couldn't help myself. I spent twenty years working for Maidenform!

VERA. Bras on the brain – oh God, my heart. *(She clutches dramatically at her chest.)*

SYLVIA. Shut up.

VERA. *(recovering immediately)* You shut up.

BRIDGET. Let me help you to the couch.

SYLVIA. I know what'll cure your heart ailments, Vera -

VERA. What?

SYLVIA. Officer Tom.

VERA. Oh! He's here? Where? Hey, kid, how do I look?

BRIDGET. Like you just chased Nana twenty blocks.

SYLVIA. You've got a little smudge right here –

> *(She starts towards* **VERA**. **VERA** *holds out her hands to stop her.)*

VERA. I'll get it! *(rubbing her face)* I must admit, I have a very strong *grandmotherly* interest in that boy.

TOM. *(enters)* Good afternoon, Sylvia. Hello Mrs. Walters. Nice to see you both.

SYLVIA. Thomas, you were so wonderful to help Bridgie with her things – such a Big, Strong Police Officer like you – you know, you're a real comfort to have around.

TOM. Hey, thanks Sylvia! I'm still kind of new on the force, you know, and the other guys sort of hassle me –

SYLVIA. No.

TOM. Yeah, 'cause they say I'm too soft. *(looks at* **BRIDGET**) I mean – that's not true or anything. I just like helping people.

SYLVIA. Of course you do, dear. Hold still just one second, you've something on your cheek. *(She removes it for him.)* Your skin is so soft! What kind of lotion do you use?

BRIDGET. *(mortified)* Nana…

SYLVIA. You come by during your break and I'll have some cookies ready for you. Bridget will help me make them, won't you Bridget?

BRIDGET. You don't bake!

SYLVIA. Well, Thomas, we don't want to keep you from your job any longer. You come by soon!

TOM. Yeah! Okay – I will. Oh, Bridge, did you need me to help you get these boxes into your room or anything?

BRIDGET. Actually, that'd be great. That one has my dishes and things in it, d'you think you could help me shove it onto the top shelf in the closet?

TOM. Yeah, sure! No problem.

(He picks up the box and moves towards the closet. SYLVIA maneuvers herself in front of the door, blocking it.)

SYLVIA. No! Nonsense! Put that box down there and don't worry about a thing.

TOM. Really, it's no problem.

SYLVIA. *(forcefully)* I don't want you to strain yourself.

BRIDGET. Nana, it's not a strain – he's actually tall enough to reach it.

SYLVIA. I'll put it up there later.

VERA. How? I thought you stopped being able to lift your arms over your head back in '98.

SYLVIA. I'll use a ladder. *(sweetly)* Now, Thomas dear, I don't want you to get in trouble. You really ought to be going.

TOM. *(confused)* Well, okay – *(He puts the box down next to the couch.)* …'bye ladies.

*(**BRIDGET** walks with him over to the front door. Opens it for him.)*

Bye Bridget.

BRIDGET. Bye Tom.

(They stand awkwardly at the door for a moment.

At the same time, **TOM** *holds out his hand for a shake and* **BRIDGET** *opens her arms for a hug. Beat. They switch,* **BRIDGET** *going for a handshake and* **TOM** *for a hug. Beat.* **TOM** *pats* **BRIDGET***'s arm, awkwardly. He exits.)*

BRIDGET. What on earth was wrong with Tom going into the closet?

SYLVIA. It's like I said! I didn't want him to strain himself. Oh, come on now, Cornflake. I wasn't embarrassing you in front of anybody – Vera probably can't even hear me.

VERA. I can, actually. I just wish I couldn't.

BRIDGET. It was just weird, that's all.

SYLVIA. Nonsense – I didn't want him to over-exhert himself! I take care of all the men in my life in special ways.

BRIDGET. Men?

SYLVIA. Yes. There's sweet little Thomas, of course. And old Mr. Tompkins, the man at the desk downstairs. I give him treats now and then, as long as he's behaving.

BRIDGET. You – what?

VERA. There are many things in that sentence you don't want to know about.

SYLVIA. And of course there's Mr. Schmidt.

BRIDGET. Who's that?

SYLVIA. Our landlord.

BRIDGET. I thought Mr. Haven was the landlord –

SYLVIA. Oh no, dear, not anymore. His son-in-law took over six or seven years ago. Mr. Schmidt.

VERA. That penny-pincher! He charges the highest rates this side of the Duck Pond – except for Sylvie, of course.

SYLVIA. I got in on the ground floor – rent control

keeps me paying a fraction of what everyone else has to. Mr. Haven never minded, but it really gets under Schmidt's skin.

BRIDGET. So how do you take care of him?

SYLVIA. I act like Vera. The more senile he thinks I am, the happier he gets. The frailer I act, the closer he thinks I'll be to that rent-free apartment in the sky. Or assisted living. I don't think he has a preference.

VERA. Nothing like the prospect of a good funeral to get people light-hearted again!

(The intercom buzzes. **SYLVIA** *crosses to it.)*

SYLVIA. Yes?

VOICE. Mrs. Charles? Your dry cleaning was just dropped off. Do you want one of the boys to run it up?

SYLVIA. My dry cleaning?

VOICE. The frilly stuff you insisted –

SYLVIA. *(Cutting him off. Loudly.)* Oh yes! Of course. Well – do you think you could –

BRIDGET. Nana, everything okay?

SYLVIA. Yes dear! Why wouldn't it be?

BRIDGET. You look worried –

VERA. She's probably constipated.

SYLVIA. Do you think you could send it up later?

VOICE. Okay, Mrs. Charles –

BRIDGET. Nana, if you don't want them to send it up, I can go get it – **(BRIDGET** *starts towards the front door.)*

SYLVIA. NO! No, dear. No. You've had a long day. You needn't run downstairs and get anything. *(to the intercom)* Yes, are you still there?

VOICE. It would seem so.

SYLVIA. I'll be right down to get it!

BRIDGET. Nana, I could –

SYLVIA. *(still at the intercom)* No!

VOICE. No you won't be down?

SYLVIA. No! No, yes I will. Be down. But wait for me. Only me! Over and out!

VOICE. 10-4, good buddy.

BRIDGET. Nana, are you sure you're okay?

SYLVIA. I am absolutely fine – but you! You look tired. Why don't you go and lie down?

BRIDGET. I'm wide-awake, Nana.

SYLVIA. Nonsense! You look tired. Doesn't she look tired, Vera?

VERA. *(didn't hear the question)* Yes, I am tired, actually.

SYLVIA. Vera, you help Bridget make up her bed and get settled in while I pop downstairs! Oh, and Bridget, see if you can find the hearing aid batteries for Vera. I keep a spare set here. *(She runs out of the apartment, slamming the door behind her.)*

VERA. *(didn't hear)* What? This damn thing keeps shorting out on me –

BRIDGET. C'mon Vera, do you know where your batteries are?

VERA. No idea. Hey kid, you want a drink?

BRIDGET. It's not even noon, Vera.

VERA. Good point. How about a Bloody Mary? *(She exits into the kitchen with her walker.)*

BRIDGET. I have a feeling this is going to be an interesting summer… Okay. Well, if I were hearing aid batteries, where would I be?

*(**BRIDGET** begins searching the living room for likely places for batteries. We hear **VERA** rattling around the kitchen. **BRIDGET** checks a small chest of drawers, the bookshelf and a few knick-knacks around the room before moving to the fireplace.)*

VERA. *(off)* CELERY?

BRIDGET. I'm sorry?

VERA. What?

BRIDGET. What did you say, Vera?

VERA. *(poking her head out of the kitchen door)* DO YOU WANT CELERY?

BRIDGET. FOR WHAT?

VERA. For what? Honestly! You don't deserve celery in your Bloody Mary! *(She's back in the kitchen.)*

(BRIDGET faces the fireplace. There are several small decorative boxes on the mantel and she opens each one looking inside for a hearing aid battery.

She opens the largest box on the upstage side of the mantle. As soon as the box is open, the faux-grate on the fireplace slides to the side.

Like a tongue, a rack of geriatric walking shoes made to look like frilly, colorful bedroom slippers rolls forward out of the fireplace.

BRIDGET does not notice, because at the same moment, there is a loud CRASH! in the kitchen.)

BRIDGET. *(turning towards the kitchen door)* VERA? Are you okay?!

(BRIDGET absentmindedly shuts the box lid, still facing the kitchen, alarmed.

The shoe display rolls back into the fireplace.

The faux-grate slides back into place.

BRIDGET pauses. Faces the audience. Beat. She looks at where the shoe display had been moments before. She looks at the audience.

CRASH! VERA rams her walker into the kitchen door.)

VERA. *(Enters with a lemonade pitcher perched on her walker and three large Santa mugs.)* Sylvie might have to get a few more glasses. I seem to have dropped a lot of them. Drink?

BRIDGET. A lot of them?

VERA. All the clean ones! *(She places the lemonade pitcher and mugs on the coffee table.)*

BRIDGET. Oh Vera, honestly. Did you clean it up?

VERA. Are you kidding me! After that death march I just took? Do you want me to have a heart attack?

BRIDGET. Fine, fine. *I'll* clean it up. *(She exits into the kitchen)*

VERA. *(She pours some Bloody Mary mix into a Santa mug and follows* **BRIDGET** *into the kitchen.)* I'll help supervise!

*(***SYLVIA*** clandestinely opens the front door and sticks her head inside. Seeing that the living room is empty, she enters and shuts the door behind her with a small snap. She is carrying a large amount of dry cleaning, all encased in see-through plastic. Every item is a lingerie article. See-thru, frilly, silky – all in a variety of colors, shapes and sizes.)*

BRIDGET. *(off)* Nana?

SYLVIA. Uh…*(looking for a place to hide things.)* Uh – yes. It's me!

BRIDGET. *(poking her head out the kitchen door)* We'll be right out. Vera sort of…

VERA. *(pulling* **BRIDGET** *back into the kitchen)* Tattle-tale!

BRIDGET. *(off, but to* **VERA***)* Just sweep the glass off the stove!

SYLVIA. Take your time!

(Frantic, **SYLVIA** *runs to the closet and opens the door. She pulls the light cord.*

Instead of a light going on, the fake panel painted to look like a closet slides to the side, out of sight behind the wall.

On a platform, the hidden interior of the closet rolls forward, similar to the fireplace, like a mechanized tongue.

The actual coat rack is attached to a pole, and is spinning slowly and of it's own accord, like a display case, or a dry-cleaner's clothing holder.*

Every article on the rack is a lingerie item. In varying shapes, sizes and colors. Enough lingerie to run a store.

SYLVIA *hurriedly begins to remove what's in the dry cleaning bags and place it on the rack. Each article has its particular place, based on color, sizing, etc.*

The phone rings.

SYLVIA *crosses to the peg-board coat rack on the downstage side of the front door. She pushes the downstage left corner of the pegboard up, tilting the whole unit so it is vertical on the wall instead of horizontal.*

The bookshelf on the upstage side of the front door swings open.

*In a hidden, slightly recessed nook – shallower than a closet – is more lingerie. This is clearly **SYLVIA**'s pink collection, as every silky article is a different shade of pink – bubblegum, rose, peach, even Barbie™ pink.*

On the back of the bookshelf unit, there is a large, full-length mirror with oversized light bulbs running around the edges of it.

The phone rings.)

BRIDGET. *(off)* Vera! Not with your bare hands! Hey, Nana? The phone's ringing!

SYLVIA. I hear it!

*(**SYLVIA** puts clothes away more quickly. She flits between the closet and the bookshelf, nervously checking to see if anyone is coming into the room while she puts the lingerie in the appropriate places.*

The phone rings.)

* See illustration on page 78. Please note that the clothes rack rotating is optional. It doesn't have to move, it just needs to exist in some form.

BRIDGET. *(off)* Nana!

SYLVIA. I know!

> (**SYLVIA** *has finished.*
>
> *She pushes the downstage right corner of the peg-board up, righting the unit so it is back in its original position. The bookshelf swings shut.*
>
> *She crosses to the closet and pulls the light cord. The platform containing the hidden interior of the closet rolls back inside. The painted panel of the fake closet slides into place.*
>
> *She shuts the closet door, holding the dry cleaning bags in her hands, unsure of where to put them. Finally, she decides to stuff them under the couch.*
>
> *The phone continues to ring.*
>
> **VERA** *enters from the kitchen and stands in the doorway. She has a dust pan in one hand and her Santa mug in the other.* **SYLVIA** *is on her hands and knees in front of the couch, 'putting the bags away.' They look at each other. Beat.)*

VERA. *(loudly and slowly, as one would say to a deaf person)* Phone. *(She exits.)*

SYLVIA. *(She gets up and grabs the portable phone on the side-table.)* Hello? Oh! Did you get my confirmation call? You didn't? I'm so sorry...No, I just called early to let you know that – *(She casts a nervous look towards the hallway).* Your order will be ready this afternoon...One-fifteen is a perfect time to drop by...Yes, the shipment came in today, and should be here well before then. I'll have everything ready for you...No! Thank *you.* I certainly appreciate your business, and I look forward to seeing you soon!

> (**SYLVIA** *hangs up.* **BRIDGET** *re-enters with* **VERA** *in tow.)*

VERA. I'm just saying that a man appreciates a woman who knows how to clean!

BRIDGET. With your coaching, I'll be a pro in no-time.

VERA. Who was on the phone?

SYLVIA. *(serving drinks)* What?

VERA. Who?

SYLVIA. Who was who? On the phone?

BRIDGET. Yes – the *phone*, Nana. Are you both deaf now?

VERA. *(didn't hear)* Huh?

SYLVIA. *(searching)* It was my bridge partner.

VERA. Your what?

SYLVIA. Bridge. Cards. She had to cancel tonight. Lost too much at Bingo the night before or something like that. Bridget, would you like a Bloody Mary?

BRIDGET. I'm good, thanks Nana.

SYLVIA. Vera? Oh, you already have –

VERA. You don't play bridge.

SYLVIA. Do you have enough celery?

VERA. I've been asking you to be my partner for *years* and I could never get you to say yes –

SYLVIA. I think I have more in the kitchen –

VERA. You've been holding out on me, haven't you?

SYLVIA. *(brightly)* Be right back!

(SYLVIA exits into the kitchen to find celery.)

VERA. I'll be damned. I bet she plays Texas hold 'em without me, too.

BRIDGET. You play poker?

VERA. Look at this face, kid. Born to bluff.

BRIDGET. I feel like this summer is going to be an interesting learning experience.

VERA. Darn tootin' it will be! Hey, move this damn box, will you. It's blocking my walker's parking space.

BRIDGET. Nana won't mind if I just shove them in the closet will she?

VERA. Shove away, kid. It'll save me having to help her later.

(**BRIDGET** *has her hand on the closet doorknob just as* **SYLVIA** *enters from the kitchen.*)

SYLVIA. What are you doing?

BRIDGET. *(with her hand still outstretched)* I was just going to put some of my boxes away –

SYLVIA. Don't be silly.

(*She swats* **BRIDGET**'s *hand away from the handle and shoos her away from the door.*)

You don't have to do that.

BRIDGET. It's really not a –

(**SYLVIA** *blocks her.*)

SYLVIA. No! I insist you leave that for later. I have something else for you to do.

BRIDGET. Nana, it's not a problem –

SYLVIA. I insist.

VERA. She insists.

BRIDGET. So I see. Okay. We can do it later.

SYLVIA. Good! Because, there's a favor I want to ask you –

VERA. I knew it. Every time I come over here I get caught up in some manual labor.

SYLVIA. Taking a walk is not manual labor.

VERA. We don't go on "walks." We go on death marches.

SYLVIA. Anyway, the manual labor isn't for you, Vera. Bridget dear, I have a picture I want hung.

BRIDGET. *("Oh God.")* Picture? Couldn't that wait until later, too? *(faking a yawn)* Whoa! All of a sudden I'm so tired!

VERA. That never works, kid.

BRIDGET. Nana, why do you want to hang up more pictures? You have so many already.

SYLVIA. I'm going for a new look in here – a new vibe. I've already started. *(She gestures to the couch where silky, rather modern looking pillows decorate the grandmotherly upholstery.)*

BRIDGET. I see – I was wondering about that...

SYLVIA. *(Exiting into the bedroom and returning a large picture frame.)* Besides, there's no such thing as too many pictures.

*(She hands **BRIDGET** the frames and crosses to the small breakfast table to get a chair, which she carries back to **BRIDGET** surveying the room.)*

Now, where do you girls think should we put this?

VERA. *(pointing)* Over there?

SYLVIA. No.

BRIDGET. *(pointing)* Over there?

SYLVIA. No.

BRIDGET & VERA. *(Both pointing in different directions.)* Over there?

SYLVIA. Right here. *(She moves towards the front door, the side with the coat rack on it.)* What do you think?

VERA. Well –

SYLVIA. It'll be perfection. Bridget, bring that chair over here?

*(**BRIDGET** slides the chair over to the wall, between the bookshelf and the pegboard.)*

BRIDGET. *(climbing up on the chair, looking at the picture)* A little racy, isn't it Nana?

SYLVIA. The female form is au natural, Muffin. Nothing scandalous about that –

VERA. Besides, you can't see any of the goods. It's all blacked out.

SYLVIA. Lift it a little higher.

VERA. More to the right.

SYLVIA. No, more to the left.

VERA. Down a little bit –

SYLVIA. Not that much!

BRIDGET. My arms are going to fall off.

SYLVIA. Vera, we need –

VERA. *(crosses to the highboy and opens a drawer to retrieve the items)* I know, I know. It's not like this is the first time we've done this.

BRIDGET. Vera – hurry.

VERA. I'll try, but after that death march today I'm feeling weak.

SYLVIA. It was not a death march! It was motivational therapy! Bridget, put it higher.

BRIDGET. I can't reach any higher.

SYLVIA. Stretch.

VERA. Here, kid.

> *(**VERA** hands **BRIDGET** a hammer and nail and crosses downstage to rest on a chair, her back to **BRIDGET**, **SYLVIA** and the bookshelf.*
>
> **BRIDGET** *places the picture on top of the coat rack, neatly resting it inside the captain's rail. She faces the wall and begins to hammer the nail in.*
>
> *The weight of the picture frame makes the pegboard tilt vertically on the wall.*
>
> *The bookshelf begins to open.*
>
> **BRIDGET** *hammers her thumb.)*

BRIDGET. OW!

SYLVIA. *(Seeing the bookshelf)* Oh no!

BRIDGET. No, it's okay. I'm okay. *(She goes back to hammering the nail into the wall.)*

(**SYLVIA** *runs to the bookshelf and forces it closed.*

The pegboard straightens on the wall. **BRIDGET** *and* **VERA** *are oblivious.*

BRIDGET, *having finally got the nail in the right spot, reaches for the picture frame. She picks it up, and puts the hammer in it's place. She turns to face the wall.*

The weight of the hammer makes the pegboard tilte vertically on the wall.

The bookshelf begins to open.

BRIDGET *can't get the picture frame to catch on the nail.*

SYLVIA *sees the bookshelf and gasps. She runs and shuts it again, just as* **VERA** *turns to look at her.*

The pegboard straights on the wall.)

VERA. What are doing? *(She stands up and crosses to the pegboard.)*

SYLVIA. *(hovering nervously by the bookshelf.)* Nothing. I'm not doing anything.

(**VERA** *looks at the pegboard, and then at* **SYLVIA**. *She pushes the downstage right corner of the pegboard, tilting it vertically on the wall.*

The bookshelf begins to open. **SYLVIA** *slams the bookshelf closed.*

The pegboard returns to its vertical position.

VERA *tilts the pegboard. The bookshelf opens.)*

SYLVIA. STOP THAT!

(**SYLVIA** *shuts the bookshelf and runs at* **VERA**. *They circle each other, waggling their fingers.* **BRIDGET** *continues to struggle with the picture frame, oblivious.*

VERA, having lured SYLVIA to her side of the room, tilts the pegboard on the wall. The bookshelf swings open before SYLVIA can get to it.

SYLVIA lets out a cry of despair just as BRIDGET manages to hang the picture and turn around. She sees the lingerie inside the bookshelf and presses herself against the wall.)

BRIDGET. WHOA! Nana? What's that?

SYLVIA. *(wildly)* That's mine!

BRIDGET. That's yours?

SYLVIA. Well, yes. Kind of.

BRIDGET. *(stumbling off her chair)* What do you mean that's yours? Nana, that is a lot of –

SYLVIA. Oh, don't ask questions, Bridget! An old woman is entitled to her little oddities.

VERA. Oddities, schmoddities. Having ten cats is odd; *this* is suspicious! *(enjoying the idea)* Did you steal this off the back of a truck?

SYLVIA. Vera! How could you accuse me of doing something like that!

VERA. *(still inspecting the coat rack peg)* I always wondered why you never let anyone hang their jackets up themselves!

BRIDGET. You never let us hang anything up...anywhere.

(Beat. BRIDGET and VERA look at the closet. SYLVIA looks nervous. As one, all three start towards the door. BRIDGET gets there first and opens it. Nothing happens.)

Is there something in the closet, Nana?

SYLVIA. Yes, it's your Christmas present. Stop snooping.

VERA. How can you see anything without turning on the light?

(VERA reaches up and yanks the light cord.

The fake panel painted to look like a closet slides to the side, out of sight behind the wall.

On a platform, the hidden interior of the closet rolls forward like a mechanized tongue, the lingerie spinning slowly on its circular rack.)

SYLVIA. Now you've gone and ruined everything.

BRIDGET. Nana, what is all this? Is it some sort of… fetish?

SYLVIA. No!

VERA. Are you running a brothel?

SYLVIA. Listen, just because I happen to have a *few* lingerie articles –

BRIDGET. A *few*? Nana, you could clothe all of the Rockettes for a slumber party and still have outfits to spare!

SYLVIA. I am not running a brothel, and I'm not clothing the Rockettes –

BRIDGET. So what exactly are you doing?

SYLVIA. *(resentfully)* Well, I wasn't going to tell you, but clearly you two busybodies have given me no choice –

VERA. Quit stalling and get to the juicy details – Do you have all of these naughty nighties for a raucous love affair you haven't told me about? I know! You're having a fling with that sculpted piece of man-meat on the force, aren't you?

BRIDGET. Let's leave Tom out of this for a minute, okay?

SYLVIA. I made all of these.

BRIDGET. Come again?

SYLVIA. I make lingerie. And then I sell it.

BRIDGET. Sell it? What do you mean by "sell it"?

SYLVIA. Oh, Bridget. You know - people come into the apartment and give me money in exchange for the lingerie. The company is actually getting quite popular –

BRIDGET. Company?

SYLVIA. Yes! "Saucy Slips, Etc."

VERA. Say that again?

SYLVIA. *(She is deaf.)* Saucy Slips, Etc.

BRIDGET. Are you kidding me? Saucy…Saucy Slips?

SYLVIA. Etc. Lingerie designed specifically with the senior citizen in mind!

BRIDGET. *(exasperated)* Why didn't you just call it Nana's Naughty Knickers?

VERA. No, no, don't change the name. Saucy Slips, Etc. has a good ring to it!

SYLVIA. *(flattered)* Thank you! I actually, I had flyers made up –

BRIDGET. For what?

SYLVIA. To hand out to people, of course. Last night was Bingo night at the Presbyterian Church down the block. I attended the festivities handed out the flyers. To my target audience! Here, I'll show you – (**SYLVIA** *disappears into her bedroom.)*

BRIDGET. *(catatonic)* I need to sit down. (**BRIDGET** *sinks onto the couch.)*

(**SYLVIA** *re-enters with a box of flyers, plops it down next to* **BRIDGET** *and hands a stack to her and* **VERA**.)

SYLVIA. Ta-da!

BRIDGET. *(reading out loud)* "Saucy Slips, Etc.: Designing lingerie that'll fire men up for a price that won't burn a hole in your wallet…"?

VERA. I don't have my damned glasses on, what's this say?

SYLVIA. *(Looks at her paper. Happily.)* No sales tax charged.

BRIDGET. You're not charging retail sales tax?

SYLVIA. No. New York sales tax is much too steep, and since I'm not giving any of the money to the government, it wouldn't be right to tax my clients.

BRIDGET. Nana, I'm almost afraid to ask you this. Do you have a license to sell things on private property?

SYLVIA. *(laughing)* Oh apple pie, you're adorable. Of course I don't!

VERA. What'd she say? I think my hearing aid just died on me –

BRIDGET. Nana!

SYLVIA. That's why Mr. Schmidt, our landlord, can't find out about any of this. He's dying for an excuse to evict me.

BRIDGET. Nana…what you're doing is illegal. You're breaking the law.

SYLVIA. Well I don't see how anyone could find out about it.

BRIDGET. You just advertised publicly at a senior citizens' Bingo game!

SYLVIA. All of my clients know perfectly well not to breathe a word to anyone. And since I never file the extra income in my taxes, I really don't –

BRIDGET. What? *(She stands up, spilling the flyers that were on her lap.)*

VERA. I actually *didn't* catch that, dear. *(fiddles with hearing aid)*

BRIDGET. Now you're breaking *several* laws. Nana, you can't do this.

SYLVIA. You see? This is why I didn't want to tell you! I knew you wouldn't understand.

VERA. Forget her – why the heck didn't you tell me Sylvie?

SYLVIA. I did, Vera. I tried to tell you. Several times. I don't think you heard me, though –

VERA. Huh? You what?

SYLVIA. I did tell you. I told when I first opened the business: I said "Vera, I'm going make lingerie for my living."

VERA. Oh! I thought you said you would make lasagna for Thanksgiving. When I never got any lasagna, well, I was disappointed. Now it all makes sense.

BRIDGET. *(is getting a headache)* How long did you say you've been…doing this?

SYLVIA. Going on six years now.

VERA. No lasagna for six years. I kept waiting!

SYLVIA. After your grandfather died I was – well, I was bored, to be perfectly honest. So I thought – "Hey, Sylvia! You know what you should do? You should get a hobby." And then I realized that I hate knitting, and I can't bake, and nothing really seemed very interesting to me – and then I thought of –

VERA. Lingerie?

SYLVIA. Exactly!

VERA. Bras on the brain –

SYLVIA. I was always happiest when I had a job, so I thought – why not make my own business? It was rocky at first, but after a few years I started to get a steady clientele, starting with one particularly good customer who has been with me since day one.

BRIDGET. Who?

VERA. *(pouting)* Well it sure as hell wasn't me. *(reflecting)* And all this time I thought those old broads you always had coming and going were part of some elaborate nude painting you were doing!

SYLVIA. Are you talking about last month, when you had to buzz in the models?

BRIDGET. Models?

SYLVIA. Yes. My "Winter Chickens"!

BRIDGET. Winter chickens?

SYLVIA. Like "Spring Chickens" … only older. They're clients of mine who have agreed to model for my web space I'm creating. It's almost ready to go up on that interweb!

BRIDGET. Wha – web space? Nana. This is all you have, right?

SYLVIA. No! There's more!

(**SYLVIA** *crosses to the fireplace and opens the largest box on the upstage side of the mantle. As soon as the box is open, the faux-grate on the fireplace slides to the side.*

Like a tongue, a rack of geriatric walking shoes made to look like frilly, colorful bedroom slippers revealed earlier.

By the bedroom door, **SYLVIA** *gives the bottom of a wall sconce a twist. A painting on the same wall swings open to reveal more bras and underwear.*)

BRIDGET. Oh my God.

VERA. Hey, Sylvie, how the heck did you get the apartment to – you know – do all this?

SYLVIA. Well, the man who lived here before Bernard and I was the building architect.

VERA. You're not talking about Moonshine Maury!

SYLVIA. The one and only! *(to* **BRIDGET***)* He was a bit of a bootlegger. During prohibition he turned the apartment into a speakeasy and –

BRIDGET. Made a few architectural improvements?

SYLVIA. Anyway, the Depression depressed Maury, and when drinking was made legal again, Maury

SYLVIA. *(cont.)* decided to move into a smaller apartment with fewer memories of the "good old days." The timing was perfect for your grandfather and I, though! We were looking for a place of our own, and we got in here for a steal.

BRIDGET. Nana – you can't do this. You cannot be doing this.

SYLVIA. Oh, don't fuss, Bridget. I *am* doing this – and doing it darn well.

BRIDGET. But –

SYLVIA. *(looking at her watch)* Now I've lost track of the time. I'm late. Listen, can I ask you both a favor?

VERA. Flavor? Chocolate for me.

BRIDGET. What kind of a favor?

VERA. *(They are deaf.)* Chocolate.

SYLVIA. I have to run downtown and go to the Golden Boys Golden Age Choir concert at the 22nd Street Retirement Villa. Business. I'm meeting my last two models there as well. Schmidt gets suspicious when too many of them meet me here. *(She removes a stack of flyers from the box. A few flutter to the floor as she crosses towards the door.)* Do you think you can hold down the fort?

BRIDGET. You mean – run the - with the racks and the –

SYLVIA. Yes. I need you both to run the store. I'm expecting a shipment to come in, and my biggest client is stopping by at one.

BRIDGET. Couldn't you just reschedule?

SYLVIA. Absolutely not. When a client wants to come, they come! And especially my big client. Mind your manners, give them anything they want, I'll probably be back before they arrive anyway.

BRIDGET. But what if something happens?

SYLVIA. What could possibly happen? *(beat)* You know, now that I think about it – it's a good thing you

two found me out. It's about time I had some
extra help around here.

VERA. You could have told me sooner, Sylvia. I would
have been happy to pitch in.

SYLVIA. *(at the door)* I know how to make it up to you,
Vera! Be my partner. We'll run this together. As
of today, the two of you are officially under the
employ of Saucy Slips, Etc. Fold some of those
flyers while I'm out!

(Exits. **VERA** *sits and starts folding flyers.)*

BRIDGET. No. No. We are not letting anyone in. She
is going to get caught and thrown into a geriatric
prison. Nobody is going to come into or leave this
apartment until we have everything sorted out and
convince her to give up this idea!

(The intercom buzzes.)

VOICE. Mrs. Charles? Officer hot-stuff is here to see
you. Should I allow him to come up?

VERA. Sure thing, sugar! *(Buzzes* **TOM** *up. Turns to look at*
BRIDGET.*)* What? Didn't you hear? We're employ-
ees now, and I have seniority on you. Get it!? *(starts
whistling* Off to Work We Go *as she uses her walker
to navigate around to the other side of the apartment*)*

BRIDGET. Vera – Tom can't come up here now!

VERA. Oh my gosh, you're right! The cookies aren't
ready yet. I'll get out those "Break 'n' Bake"
squares – you fire up the oven!

BRIDGET. Vera! No! Help me hide all of this!

VERA. Oh, Tom won't mind a little mess. Where the
hell does Sylvia keep those baking sheets?

(knock on front door)

Coming!

BRIDGET. NO! *(Flings herself in front of the door. Whispers.)*
We have to put the flyers and the slips away.

*Please see Music Use Note on Page 3.

VERA. What?

BRIDGET. *(still whispering)* The flyers! The slips!

VERA. WHAT?

BRIDGET. JUST PUT THE COOKIES IN THE OVEN!

VERA. Oh! Right! *(wheels around with her walker and goes back into the kitchen)*

BRIDGET. *(talking to the door)* Just a second. We had a little – problem. *(starts frantically stuffing flyers back into the box)* A big problem.

TOM. Bridget, please open up. This is serious.

BRIDGET. Just a second! Vera's getting your cookies ready!

TOM. *(knocking louder on the door)* Bridget!

VERA. You still haven't let Romeo in? I'll get it.

BRIDGET. *(frantic)* What about the cookies?!

VERA. I already put 'em under the broiler. They'll be ready in no time!

BRIDGET. The broiler – Vera, you can't put cookies in the broiler!

VERA. You should fix your hair, kid, you look a little crazy.

> *(**VERA** crosses to front door. At the same time **BRIDGET** is running around the apartment trying to make everything go back into place. Just as the bookshelf is sliding shut, **VERA** reaches the door and opens it. Flyers are still strewn over the floor. **TOM** enters. **VERA** exits back into the kitchen.)*

BRIDGET. Heeeeey!

TOM. Are you still unpacking?

BRIDGET. Unpacking? Nope. Re-packing. *(She drops to the floor and begins stuffing flyers back into the box.)*

TOM. You're repacking your boxes?

BRIDGET. What boxes? *(Looks at the box in her hand. Looks at the boxes **TOM** carried in earlier. They are* *identical)* Oh! *Those* boxes! Yes. I am. I am unpacking *my* boxes.

TOM. Well, do you think you could do it a bit more quickly?

BRIDGET. I thought I –

TOM. It's just that – it's illegal, you know. *(Sits on the couch next to a stack of flyers. He drums his fingers on them, annoyed.)*

BRIDGET. What? Illegal? Don't be silly! Ha-ha! Nothing illegal's going on here. Just my boxes with my things in them! *(trying to move the flyers away from him)*

TOM. It *is* illegal, Bridget. And…and I'm really sorry, and I'm not angry or anything, but I *did* ask you to move the car. And…and if you don't…well, I might have to give you a –

VERA. *(entering from kitchen)* Cookie? Don't mind the crunch, they're supposed to be blackened like that. It's good for your teeth…or eyes…or something.

BRIDGET. The car? Oh! I haven't moved my car!

TOM. I know!

BRIDGET. Oh, Tom, I'm so sorry. I'll go run down and do it right now. *(places the box with the flyers behind the couch. There are still loose flyers on the sofa.)*

TOM. Okay, good. Because there was a lot of swearing going on down there, and if anyone calls in to the station to complain they're going to –

BRIDGET. No, I understand. I'll do that now. And you should go.

VERA. Go? He hasn't even eaten one cookie yet! I'll get milk. Sit down, Tom.

*(*TOM *is about to sit on the couch, next to the box with the flyers.)*

BRIDGET. NO! Not there!

(**TOM** *stops mid-sit and awkwardly straightens back up.*)

BRIDGET. *(cont.)* Uh, I think my keys are there.

(He turns around to help her look. She throws her keys across the room. He goes to pick them up.)

THANKS! You...uh...help with the – milk.

*(She pushes **TOM** towards **VERA**. **VERA** catches him, overjoyed, and grabs his butt. then she pulls him into the kitchen.)*

Okay. Let's...camouflage!

(She puts the flyers in with a stack of her own boxes, places another box on top of it, and drapes all of them with a blanket from the couch.)

Perfect. *(to kitchen)* I'm just going to run downstairs and move the car.

(**BRIDGET** *exits out the front door, leaving it open behind her. She turns to the left, where the stairs are. A small pause, then the 'ding!' of an elevator and* **MR. SCHMIDT**, *an overbearing man in his 60s, enters from the right.*)

TOM. *(enters from kitchen)* You're right, the charred taste goes away with the milk. Kind of. Oh. Hey, Mr. Schmidt.

MR. SCHMIDT. Officer? *(excited)* Don't tell me – she's finally died, hasn't she? Yes?

TOM. *(mouth full)* Naw, buht Vewra made thome cookie. Wan' won?

MR. SCHMIDT. No. *(beat)* Where the hell is Mrs. Charles?

TOM. Sylvia?

VERA. *(entering from kitchen.)* Hey copper, I found one that isn't quite as – Schmitty.

MR. SCHMIDT. Mrs. Walters. *(awkward pause)* Everything's fine in your apartment?

VERA. Everything's great except the fact my husband's still there. But since you're only the landlord, you can't fix that for me, can you?

MR. SCHMIDT. I see today is sarcastic day. Wonderful. Now look here, Mrs. Walters, where's your friend? We've got a few things to discuss.

VERA. What did you say?

MR. SCHMIDT. Mrs. Charles – where's Mrs. Charles?

VERA. Huh? Charlie who? Speak up.

MR. SCHMIDT. SYLVIA CHARLES.

VERA. WHAT ABOUT HER?

MR. SCHMIDT. WHERE IS SHE?

VERA. Haven't the faintest. *(exits into the kitchen)*

TOM. I think I should –

MR. SCHMIDT. No, you wait a minute. Are you on duty now?

TOM. Yes, and I really ought to–

MR. SCHMIDT. No. I need your help. There's been a lot of funny business going around my apartment building and I want to put an end to it, once and for all.

TOM. You mean break-ins?

MR. SCHMIDT. Well, in a sense. You see, a lot of visitors have been coming and going – and *not* checking in at the desk downstairs. *Elderly* visitors, and – are you gonna write this down, or what?

TOM. Oh! Right, of course. *(fumbles for notebook)* Has anyone reported anything missing?

MR. SCHMIDT. Well – no. But several noise complaints have been filed and a few residents have told me that they've had to buzz in strangers who were trying to visit *this* apartment.

TOM. Well, that's not a crime, really, sir.

MR. SCHMIDT. No, but it's fishy! What's an 83 year-old doing with a so many *old* friends? They have to start dying after a while, right?

TOM. Well, I'm not sure. Vera was just telling me that Sylvia's been working this nude –

SCHMIDT. And then there are all of those goddamn deliveries.

TOM. Deliveries?

SCHMIDT. Yeah, and they keep getting bigger. I don't know what she has shipped here all the time, but I just got a call from the desk man today saying UPS called about her boxes arriving earlier than expected and how they'd bring them over today.

TOM. I'm afraid I don't –

MR. SCHMIDT. Funny business, don't you see?

TOM. Kind of?

SCHMIDT. *(more to himself)* She thinks she can walk all over me, just because she has a rent-controlled apartment –

TOM. It's great, isn't it? Living smack in the middle of New York for a fraction of the cost.

SCHMIDT. Yeah. It's wonderful! You know what's really great?

TOM. What?

SCHMIDT. It's really great that her rent doesn't cover the heating bill for the month of December. I love eating the cost of that! I *love* spending money that I wouldn't HAVE to spend if some hotshot socialite moved in and paid me the NORMAL rent! But no. Do I have a socialite? No. I have Sylvia Charles, who has been here for 60 years and hasn't died yet.

TOM. Still kicking. *(toasts* **SYLVIA** *with the burnt cookie)*

SCHMIDT. There are a lot of bad people in the world. And there are all different kinds of thieves – *someone* here is taking advantage of New York City zoning laws, and worse – of me!

TOM. Really? *(enjoying this)* Who?

SCHMIDT. Are you following me?

TOM. *(teasing)* Sure I am. You're worried that someone might try to take advantage of Sylvia because she has a rent-controlled apartment. Right?

SCHMIDT. I – no –

TOM. *(playing with him)* But you don't think that somebody could take advantage of an 83 year-old woman? Who would be cold-blooded enough to try to extort her in some way?

SCHMIDT. Well – you never know.

TOM. Tell you what, how about I help you? I'll keep an eye on the apartment and I'll let you know if I see anything suspicious going on –

SCHMIDT. Really? *(Feels as though the tables have been turned but can't figure out exactly how that happened. Trying to regain control.)* Good. You do that. Here's my card. I want you to call me if anything happens – if people come over to visit, if she gets something in the mail, what time she leaves to walk the dog –

TOM. She doesn't have a dog –

SCHMIDT. Just do a little detective work.

TOM. I'll do that. *(happily and conversationally)* I always dreamed of being a detective, ever since I read those Hardy Boys books when I was a kid.

MR. SCHMIDT. Well that's nice, I guess. Just remember to call me if any funny business goes on here. *(exits out front door, turns to the right)*

TOM. *(calling after him)* Sure thing! Anything to help out Sylvia!

VERA. *(off, from kitchen)* HEY! I can't hear a damned thing. What's going on in there? Has Schmitty vacated the premises yet?

TOM. Yeah! He's gone.

VERA. *(enters)* Boy, sometimes *I* can't even tell when I actually can't hear something, or if I'm just doing it to get Schmidty's goat.

*(***BRIDGET*** enters, out of breath and shuts the front door behind her.)*

BRIDGET. Parking in this city is murder! Took me ten minutes just to make it around the block – *(Sees* **TOM**. *Horrified.)* Tom? What are you still doing here?

TOM. Oh – I – had a cookie. And then the landlord came by...

VERA. Yeah, what did Schmidt want, anyway?

TOM. Uh – just to talk. That was all. He mentioned something about a package.

BRIDGET. A package? What kind of package?

TOM. He didn't say – just that it was a large shipment and –

BRIDGET. Oh God.

VERA. I'll get you another glass of milk.

BRIDGET. Tom, you really should go. Don't want you to get in trouble with the boys for, you know, fraternizing with us normal citizens.

*(***BRIDGET*** propels him towards the door, **VERA** following in tow with the tray of burnt cookies perched on the top of her walker and a glass of milk in one hand.)*

Really great seeing you, take a few of these for the road. *(grabs a handful of cookies and pushes them towards him while opening the door behind him)* Bye Tom! *(slams the door shut)*

TOM. *(off)* Bye.

VERA. Did you park the car, kid?

BRIDGET. God, no. I couldn't find a space so I just double-parked again a few blocks down. Did you hear what they were talking about?

VERA. What kind of stupid question is that?

BRIDGET. A big delivery? For Nana? You don't think it has anything to do with –

VERA. Saucy Slips? I'll lay odds ten to one that it does.

BRIDGET. Vera, sit down. Before anything else happens I need you to be on the same page as me. What Nana is doing is illegal.

(**BRIDGET** *guides* **VERA** *over to the couch.*)

VERA. You worry too much. Besides, if we get in any trouble you can look in your law books and find one of those doughnut holes!

BRIDGET. It doesn't work like that! She could go to jail for tax evasion, selling without a vendor's license… being crazy! Please just promise me you won't let anyone else in the apartment, okay?

VERA. Jail? For tax evasion?

BRIDGET. That's how they got Al Capone.

VERA. He died of syphilis, you know.

BRIDGET. Vera – focus! Nobody can come up here!

VERA. Not even Tom?

BRIDGET. Absolutely not. Especially not Tom.

VERA. Fine. But I have to give him the rest of his cookies somehow.

(**SYLVIA** *bursts in through the front door.*)

SYLVIA. The spit has hit the fan.

BRIDGET. What happened?

VERA. If there's any more excitement in store for today, I'm taking my nap now.

SYLVIA. Vera, you can sleep when you're dead. This is serious.

BRIDGET. If it doesn't involve the police or the IRS, I don't want to hear about it.

SYLVIA. No. Something worse. Both of my models had to go to the doctor today!

BRIDGET. What?

SYLVIA. I know! It's terrible!

BRIDGET. Well – are they okay?

SYLVIA. Oh they're fine. The retirement home served sauerkraut last night and they both came down with bad gas, but now I don't have anyone to model my last four outfits – the most important ones, too! They complete my entire line and I wanted to get them up on my webspace today so I could finally launch the site.

BRIDGET. *(sarcastic)* Well, too bad you can't get your website up. I feel awful. Really, too bad. Maybe you should scratch that idea all together and just not advertise on the internet at all. Or maybe just not do any advertising. That would probably be best.

SYLVIA. And give in to defeat? Not a chance! You see, I was distressed at first –

VERA. Understandably so.

SYLVIA. But then I realized I had the perfect model right in my own home. She's beautiful, she's funny, she looks great in red –

VERA. You convinced me. I'll do it.

BRIDGET. No way.

VERA. Listen, I was the cat's meow when I was your age, and my legs still look pretty darn good – don't they Sylvie?

SYLVIA. They don't look a day over 60, Vera. So you'll do it?

VERA. Of course I will! Show me to my dressing room! And who will be the second model?

SYLVIA. Oh…well –

VERA. Sylvia, you must! Think of your art!

SYLVIA. I don't know, Vera. I love lingerie, but I haven't put any on since my husband –

VERA. Man up, woman!

BRIDGET. Nana, I love you and Vera dearly, but I don't think I want to see either one of you in –

SYLVIA. Bridget, we need you! I need you to take the pictures! And for support!

VERA. Bridget should wear lingerie, too!

BRIDGET/SYLVIA. What?

VERA. Sure! Why not? Camaraderie! Emotional support. Etc, etc.

BRIDGET. Nana, I am not modeling some obscene lingerie for your website.

SYLVIA. Well, no offense darling, but my line isn't really targeted to your generation. Vera and I will be the models…I'm just nervous about doing it! Vera's right, I need you to do this with us. I need your support.

VERA. C'mon, Kid! This'll make a good story, one day.

SYLVIA. Please Bridget? It'll be such fun! And I'm curious to see what my designs would look like on a younger gal anyway!

VERA. You could start to branch out to the under-60s set, Sylvie!

BRIDGET. Oh God.

VERA. Good! She'll do it! Let's get this show on the road.

SYLVIA. Here, you take these – *(She reaches into her large tote and pulls out a few brightly colored lingerie items and hands them to* **VERA.***)* and go try them on in the bedroom. Oh, wait. You've got a little something right here – *(moves to grab* **VERA***'s cheek)*

BRIDGET. Nana, this is –

SYLVIA. Bridget, you know what your problem is? You don't have enough fun.

BRIDGET. Well excuse me if my idea of fun doesn't include…. Saucy Slips and tax evasion!

SYLVIA. Hush, Bridget. I'm not a young woman any-more, and I realize that I don't have a whole hell of a lot of time to enjoy life. So I'm going to do what I want to do while I can still do it! I'm not hurting anybody. To hell with all these little problems you keep yapping about. Now be a good girl. Make your old grandmother happy and put on this.

(She hands **BRIDGET** *a few silky articles from the same bag.)*

BRIDGET. But I…

SYLVIA. It's not hurting anyone and I need you. Really, I do.

BRIDGET. Fine! Ugh! *(Storms off into the bathroom. Slams the door.)*

*(***VERA** *dramatically flings open the bedroom door and leans against the frame. She is dressed in a dress slip – knee length, bright green, with a v-neck and a slit that runs from her knee-cap up to mid thigh. She's got her walker with her, too.)*

VERA. I'm ready for my close-up! *(walks towards the couch "sexily," humming* One Singular Sensation.*)*

BRIDGET. *(off)* Nana!

SYLVIA. What, dear?

BRIDGET. *(off)* This won't work!

SYLVIA. Why on earth not?

BRIDGET. *(Opens bathroom door and stands, sulking. The slip is much too big for her in the chest area, clearly designed for someone with large breasts. She points to her chest and says nothing.)*

VERA. You must wear some heavy-duty push-up bras, kid. I never noticed you were built like a flapper!

SYLVIA. Oh dear! I suppose I do give a little more room in the bust. Us older gals –

*See Music Use Note on page 3.

BRIDGET. Nana.

VERA. Put yours on, Sylvie!

SYLVIA. Right-o! *(She exits into the bathroom with another piece of lingerie.)*

BRIDGET. Nana. This is too embarrassing. I'm going to go take this off.

SYLVIA. *(off)* You will do nothing of the sort. You look wonderful, Bridget!

VERA. I know what'll make you feel better!

*(**VERA** takes off her socks, rolls them up and stuffs them down **BRIDGET**'s front. Adjusts them from the outside.)*

There! That's much better.

BRIDGET. Oh great. Much better.

*(**SYLVIA** emerges from the bathroom in a bright red slip, knee length, with boa feathers at the bottom and top.)*

VERA. *(wolf-whistles)* Hey Angel-Cake! Where are we going to set up shop?

SYLVIA. I was actually thinking in the study might be a good idea.

VERA. I like it! Sort of lounging in an arm chair like so – *(dramatic pose)* – with a book –

SYLVIA. Or a pipe!

VERA. A pipe! I like it!

BRIDGET. Playboy for pensioners. What a novel idea.

SYLVIA. Grab the camera in my bag, Bridie, and let's rock and roll!

*(**SYLVIA** and **VERA** exit into the hallway upstage right.)*

BRIDGET. *(adjusts the socks)* I need a drink.

(Moves towards kitchen. Intercom buzzes. She stops.)

Oh God.

VOICE. *(over intercom)* Mrs. Charles? Your packages arrived, and I must say you were not forthright in revealing the quantity of this particular delivery.

BRIDGET. He'll go away. I won't answer and he'll just go away with his stupid boxes.

VOICE. Mrs. Charles? Mrs. Charles? *(louder)* VERA WAL-TERS? ARE YOU THERE?

BRIDGET. *(whispering)* Nobody here. Return everything. Have it returned.

VOICE. Well, I'm not sure if you can hear this or not – but Officer Good Looking was down here a few minutes ago who said he'd come back and help the UPS Men unload, so –

BRIDGET. NO! *(runs to the intercom)* No! Hi!…hi. I'm Bridget. Sylvia's granddaughter. Don't leave them with Tom. Why don't *you* just bring them up? Or *anyone* but Officer Good Looking. *(buzzes him in)* NANA? What exactly is in that shipment you were expecting today?

SYLVIA. *(entering)* Oh, is it here already?

BRIDGET. Yes – and Tom is offering to help us unpack it.

SYLVIA. That's sweet of him, but Tom shouldn't see the merchandise. He wouldn't understand – he doesn't have anyone to buy unmentionables for.

BRIDGET. Nana, what *are* you expecting?

(knock on the door)

SYLVIA. Oh, some more flyers, a few dressmakers' dummies, bolts of fabric and a few slips I designed and had sent out to a sewing company. My big client placed a huge order a few weeks ago and I didn't have the manpower to get it filled by today – so I out-sourced!

*(**SYLVIA** crosses and opens the door. **UPS MAN** enters with seven large boxes piled on the moving dolly.)*

Oh thank you, dear. Would you like some cookies and milk?

UPS MAN. *(sees* **BRIDGET***)* YEAH!

SYLVIA. This is my granddaughter –

UPS MAN. She's here all summer?

SYLVIA. Yes –

UPS MAN. Thank you God.

SYLVIA. Where are the rest of my boxes?

UPS MAN. *(distracted)* Uh – downstairs –

SYLVIA. Go get them, dear.

(He exits, walking backwards. **BRIDGET** *has gone to the nearest box and opened it.)*

BRIDGET. Nana, these are from your sewing company, but – oh my god.

SYLVIA. What? Are they too wonderful for words?

BRIDGET. Nana, they're pornographic!

SYLVIA. *(taking one of the flyers from the top)* Don't be silly, my taste level is very – oh dear! Well, I certainly did not order that. What is that man doing?

BRIDGET. And this one?

SYLVIA. Absolutely not. This isn't even the color scheme I ordered.

VERA. *(entering from the hallway, with walker, crosses to* **BRIDGET** *and* **VERA***)* What have we here, ladies? Some more slips for me to model or –

*(***BRIDGET** *hands her a flier.)*

Sylvia, I refuse to pose like this.

SYLVIA. These aren't mine! What does this packing slip say? Saucy…lips? Saucy Lips?

BRIDGET. *(continuing to read)* "Boldly going where no lips have gone before"? And there's a website, too.

SYLVIA. But my site hasn't even launched yet!

BRIDGET. No, Nana. I think there was a mistake. the sewing company must have switched your order with someone else's. *(opening another box and pulling out a whip and a pair of handcuffs)* Unless your big client is into S&M, we might have a problem here.

SYLVIA. No! This is terrible! *(Frantically starts opening the other boxes. She throws out items from each box – more fliers, fish-net tights, belts, wigs, handcuffs, etc.)*

(Loud knock on door. **BRIDGET** *rises and opens it.* **UPS MAN** *enters with a* **SECOND UPS MAN.** *They stand in the doorway.* **SYLVIA** *and* **VERA,** *in their own world, are holding up Saucy Lips products, trying them on and giggling like schoolgirls. Bridget waves a mannequin bust with pointy, leather covered breasts at the* **UPS MEN.** *)*

BRIDGET. I think there was some sort of mistake – everything got switched around – so if you could just, you know, take these away and bring back the boxes that we ordered – or actually, don't bring back *anything.* Just take these away…

(The **UPS MEN** *and* **VERA** *and* **SYLVIA** *notice each other at the same time. The ups men drop their boxes, shocked!)*

UPS MAN. *(recovering)* I only bring in, I don't take out. Unless it's you. On a date. I'll get the cookies later, Mrs. Charles! And, hey – nice nightie. *(Pinches* **BRIDGET***'s silk-covered bottom. To* **VERA.***)* Wow. Kinky. *(exits, slamming the door behind him)*

SYLVIA. My client is coming in 40 minutes! What are we going to do?

VERA. We will sew!

SYLVIA. We will?

VERA. Sure. I'm better at that machine than you are anyway. We have fabric here. We'll do our best to get the order done, and see what happens.

BRIDGET. You can't just –

VERA. Bridget, it's time you stopped raining on our picnic. You're either in or out.

SYLVIA. Please Bridget? It's the most important customer I have – and to imagine I'd be a disappointment…after six years?

BRIDGET. Fine! Let's just get this over with. We have to –

(loud knock on the front door)

TOM. *(Off. Sharply.)* Bridget? Open up.

BRIDGET. What's wrong Tom?

TOM. *(off)* I found your car double-parked. *Again.* And I'm sorry, but I have to give you a ticket. Open up!

(All three women look at each other, then the mess on the floor, then the outfits that they are wearing.)

BRIDGET, **SYLVIA**, **VERA.** *(Sing-song.)* Just a minute!

(As one, all make a mad dash to start cleaning up until –

Blackout)

ACT TWO

(Immediately following. **BRIDGET**, **SYLVIA** *and* **VERA** *scatter to hide boxes, papers and cloth.* **SYLVIA** *goes to the coat rack by the front door and pushes one corner to tilt the rack vertically on the wall. The bookshelf on the other side of the door swings open.* **SYLVIA** *shoves whips and chains inside.* **BRIDGET** *follows suit; she carries lingerie over and piles them in.* **VERA**, *meanwhile, has been stuffing flyers, bras and panties beneath couch cushions and* **TOM** *has not stopped knocking on the door. He alternates between knocks and doorbell rings. He is annoyed and speaks throughout the "clean-up" taking place on-stage.)*

TOM. Bridget. Sylvia. Open this door…I know you're there. I can hear you…*(beat. child-like.)* …Are you there?… Please open up. I know you don't want a ticket, but it's not that big of a deal…Bridget!… Hey, I can reduce the fine, you know – maybe… but only if you answer right now. *(whining)* C'mon guys…

VERA. There! *(She has finished stuffing the couch. Edges of papers protrude from all sides. The tail of a whip lays over the arm of the couch. Fuzzy handcuffs are visible.)*

SYLVIA. *(Pushing the peg. The bookshelf swings shut.)* You have to get him out of here, Bridget!

BRIDGET. How can I get him out if we haven't even let him in, yet?

(She runs a stack of boxes over to the bedroom, shoves them in, slams the door. She runs back to the last box, picks it up, runs to the bathroom door, opens it, throws the box inside and slams the door. Looks down and realizes she's still in a slip. Loudly.)

BRIDGET. *(cont.)* OH!

TOM. Bridget? Are you okay?

BRIDGET. *(to* **TOM***)* NO! *(whispering)* Nana, I can't open the door dressed like this!

SYLVIA. *(to* **TOM***)* She's fine!

BRIDGET. *(to the room)* No I'm not!

VERA. *(throwing a knitted blanket at her)* There you go, kid! Do like the Romans do.

BRIDGET. If you start chanting "Toga!" I am jumping out the window.

TOM. Bridget! Sylvia! VERA!

VERA. Copper's getting cranky – even I heard that one.

TOM. Bridget, if you don't answer the door by the time I count to five, I'm doubling the fine!

SYLVIA. *(helping* **BRIDGET** *with the blanket)* Get rid of him while Vera and I start recreating the order.

TOM. One…

BRIDGET. But how?

TOM. Two…

SYLVIA. Try talking yourself out of the ticket while you talk *him* out the door.

BRIDGET. And if that doesn't work?

TOM. Three…

VERA. Yell.

BRIDGET. Yell? At Tom?

TOM. Four…

VERA. Works with my husband. I start shouting and – pft! – like a racehorse out of the gates. Good luck, kid.

BRIDGET. Don't leave me alone with him!

TOM. Four and one-eighth…

SYLVIA. You'll be fine. Get him out fast. C'mon, Vera – let's get sewing!

(SYLVIA and VERA exit into the bedroom.)

TOM. Four and one-fourth…

(BRIDGET runs to the door and pulls it open.)

TOM. Four and two – about time!

BRIDGET. I'm really sorry, I was just –

TOM. *(Clearly agitated, he walks past her into the apartment.)* One of the other cops saw your car, you know.

BRIDGET. Oh?

TOM. Yeah. We graduated from the academy together. I was ahead of him in our class. "Old Eagle Eyes." That's what they called me.

BRIDGET. *(She notices "Saucy Lips" bright gold bustier on the couch and edges towards it, panicked.)* Eagle Eyes?

TOM. So he radios me – "Hey, Eagle Eyes, looks like you missed a big fat Violation 14 – B on your beat –" Well of course I didn't miss it. I saw it. I told you to move your car!

(BRIDGET picks up the bustier and holds it to her chest. TOM looks at her. Quick beat. He keeps talking, not even registering what he saw. BRIDGET stuffs the bustier into the couch cushions and tries to frantically stuff it as far in as it will go.)

But I'll tell you one thing, Bridget. Ol' Eagle Eyes doesn't miss anything. I got top marks in street scenario. TOP marks. It's just now he's gone and radioed me about it, which means dispatch heard. Which means my boss heard. So I have to give you a ticket.

(He takes out his ticket book and begins writing. BRIDGET awkwardly crosses over to him, making a brave attempt at seduction.)

BRIDGET. I don't suppose I could talk you out of doing that?

TOM. *(Seeing her for the first time.)* What are you wearing?

BRIDGET. I – just go out of the shower?

TOM. You dried yourself off with a wool afgan?

BRIDGET. I sure did.

TOM. Oh. Okay. Here. *(hands her the ticket)* Listen, I'm sorry about this. *(sits on the couch)* It's just that I – *(he absent-mindedly picks up the fuzzy handcuffs and begins twiddling with them)*

BRIDGET. *(Sees the handcuffs. Yelling.)* Just what do you think you're doing!?

TOM. Huh? *(he drops the fuzzy cuffs)*

BRIDGET. You think you can sit on my – on my Nana's couch like that, after fining me!

TOM. What?

BRIDGET. *(wildly)* What kind of girl do you think I am!

TOM. *(Stands and moves towards* **BRIDGET.***)* Bridge, I'm sorry that I –

BRIDGET. *(getting into it)* Don't you 'Bridge' me! I'm angry!

TOM. Angry?

BRIDGET. Yes?

TOM. But you blocked an entire street for 45 minutes after I already asked you to move your car –

BRIDGET. *(backing him towards the front door, getting angrier)* Don't try to spin this around on me! You come in here with your stupid cop outfit and your "I sure love to help people" stuff and – and- and you eat my Nana's famous cookies and –

TOM. They were Break and Bake. I saw the wrapper. And Vera actually –

BRIDGET. You act all nice and now this? *(waving the ticket wildly)* THIS?

TOM. I had to!

BRIDGET. Leave! Get out of here! I'll never forgive you – ever!

*(She backs **TOM** into the wall. On her last line, she pokes him in the chest, hard, and his shoulder nudges the peg board so that it tilts vertically against the wall. The bookshelf swings open. **TOM** does not notice. **BRIDGET** does.)*

TOM. Listen, Bridget – you're really over-reacting!

*(To stop him from noticing, **BRIDGET** grabs **TOM** by the lapels and makes him face her again.)*

BRIDGET. I know I am!

(She pulls him into a kiss while at the same time opening the door behind him. She shoves him out into the hallway, yells:)

Come back tomorrow when I don't hate you! *(And slams the door. She looks at the ticket.)* Five dollars? *(Throws the blanket onto the floor and angrily straightens the coat rack on the wall. The bookshelf closes.)* Great! Well, there's another guy that thinks I'm insane. Maybe I am insane. I'm talking to myself – that's a sign of crazy. I need a drink. NANA! Is there more of that Bloody Mary crap?

SYLVIA. *(off)* In the fridge dear, in the lemonade pitcher!

BRIDGET. Of course it is. *(exits to kitchen, muttering)*

SYLVIA. *(enters from bedroom with a brassiere on over her slip, frantic)* Bridget, does this bow here look right to you?

BRIDGET. *(off)* Not now, Nana.

SYLVIA. Vera says it's just the right amount of saucy, but I –

BRIDGET. *(re-entering with a Bloody Mary in one hand and a bottle of vodka in the other)* Tom fined me five dollars and I yelled at him like a lunatic.

SYLVIA. It just doesn't go with the look. VERA! Take this damn bow off.

BRIDGET. Are you listening to me? I got your crazy genes.

SYLVIA. VERA! *(trying to unhook the bra but can't)* Oh damnit. Vera! Get in here.

BRIDGET. I kissed him, too. Our first kiss was instigated because I'm a bi-polar nut trying to hide the bookshelf full of sex-kitten outfits. *(to herself)* Sex-cat? What would you call them when they're for grandmothers?

SYLVIA. *(still struggling with the bra)* This is why I stopped wearing these years ago. Damn! Help me, Bridget.

BRIDGET. *(helping* **SYLVIA** *undo the bra)* I'll never have a boyfriend at this rate.

SYLVIA. That's nice dear. Vera! The clasp you put on is faulty.

*(***VERA*** enters from the bedroom. She is dressed in her silky negligee, but now she has a pin cushion on one arm, a tape measure around her neck, scissors and a strip of mesh-like fabric from the Saucy Lips order in hand.)*

VERA. What the hell do you want?

SYLVIA. Your craftsmanship is shoddy.

VERA. Listen, baby, just 'cause you're tense doesn't mean you have to take it out on the help.

SYLVIA. I am not tense.

VERA. You're tense.

SYLVIA. I'm not.

VERA. You are.

BRIDGET. Drink?

SYLVIA. Yes.

BRIDGET. Thanks. *(she takes a swig from the vodka bottle)*

VERA. What did that hunka-hunka-burnin' love want?

BRIDGET. I have to move the car again. What he fails to realize is there is NO parking in Manhattan. That, and that my grandmother is running an illegal lingerie ring and has to be babysat so she doesn't get thrown in the slammer. *(takes a long swig from the bottle)*

VERA. No parking? What a crock! I know the perfect place to park. Give me the keys and I'll take care of everything.

BRIDGET. Wonderful. Here, Vera, here are the keys.

VERA. Right! I'm off! *(She takes the keys, grabs her walker and starts valiantly towards the door.)*

BRIDGET. Vera!

VERA. Don't stop me now, kid – my momentum is up!

BRIDGET. Vera. You're in a negligee.

VERA. Right. Change first, drive the car later.

BRIDGET. Right.

*(**VERA** exits into the bedroom.)*

SYLVIA. *(sinking onto the sofa)* We're never going to be able to finish the order on time.

BRIDGET. Don't you think your big client would understand?

SYLVIA. I'm sure she would, Bridget, but I've gone six years without messing up.

BRIDGET. Well, you're a talented businesswoman, Nana. A bit unorthodox, perhaps, and with no regard to laws or the idea of jail time – but a talented businesswoman all the same.

SYLVIA. Thank you, Sweet Cakes. Your grandfather always used to say that, too.

BRIDGET. Did he?

SYLVIA. Sure did. I used to work for a brassiere company back in the forties – gave the economy a lift just like it did for the women!

BRIDGET. Suddenly everything makes sense.

*(**VERA** re-enters, now wearing her original outfit as well as the pincushion and tape measure.)*

VERA. Now I'm off!

SYLVIA. Bon-voyage.

VERA. Listen, Sylvie, when I get back I want to see a serious improvement in morale, okay?

SYLVIA. Okay, okay.

VERA. We'll get through this! It's just like the Va-va-va-Vunderbra mix-up of '78! We got through that fine.

SYLVIA. You're right, Vera. I almost forgot!

VERA. Then onward-ho! *(She exits, slamming the door behind her.)*

SYLVIA. *(about to explain the mixup of '78)* We –

BRIDGET. I'm good. I don't want to know.

SYLVIA. Yes. Well, perhaps that's for the best. You're a bit young, still.

BRIDGET. Nana, why did you start working for Maidenform? I mean, Grandpa made a lot of money…

SYLVIA. Free girdles. And I was bored.

BRIDGET. And when Grandpa died – ?

SYLVIA. Bridget, I've never been very good at just sitting around and twiddling my thumbs. I liked being a salesgirl with Maidenform and decided to stick with what I know! Enough questions. Take this damn bow off.

*(**SYLVIA** hands the bra to **BRIDGET**. There is a knock on the door.)*

SYLVIA. I'll get it. *(Opens the door. It is **VERA**).*

VERA. I forgot my glasses.

SYLVIA. Your glasses?

VERA. I can't drive without my glasses.

SYLVIA. You didn't wear glasses today.

VERA. I didn't?

SYLVIA. You didn't.

BRIDGET. Vera, get going! tom is upset enough already.

VERA. Right – not to worry. I am on-task! *(exits, slamming the door behind her)*

SYLVIA. Oh, Pumpkin Seed, I don't think Tom was all that upset.

BRIDGET. He was acting like it.

(There is a knock on the front door)

SYLVIA. Goodness! *(She opens the door. It is* **VERA**. *Again.)* Now what?

VERA. I forgot to ask –

BRIDGET. It's parked on 67th between Lexington and Third.

VERA. Perfect. *(***VERA** *exits.* **SYLVIA** *slams the door behind her this time.)*

SYLVIA. You know, with all of this going wrong, it's really making me start to rethink the whole business move.

BRIDGET. Oh thank God! Maybe you should just shut the store down and take up a new hobby. What about Mary Kay? That's harmless…are they still giving away cars?

SYLVIA. Why do one when I can do both? Though I'll need more help than Vera. Having you here has made me realize that. *(beat)* Bridget, do you think you'd want to –

BRIDGET. I'm good. Law school.

SYLVIA. Okay, then.

(A knock on the front door.)

Vera –

BRIDGET. I wonder what she forgot this time?

SYLVIA. Probably her dentures.

BRIDGET. I'll get it this time, Nana. You take a pair of scissors to the bra.

SYLVIA. Wonderful idea. I'll be at the ol' machine if you need me! *(She exits into the bedroom.)*

BRIDGET. *(to herself)* Wonderful.

*(**BRIDGET** crosses to the front door and opens it. In the doorway is **HEATHER**, a young, bubblegum chewing 'spokeswoman' for Saucy Lips. She is clad – if one can call it that – in a fun mish-mosh of denim, fishnet and 100% American-grown cotton. **HEATHER** should look as if she might charge a fair hourly rate. **BRIDGET** slams the door, and leans against it.)*

BRIDGET. Ok. Let me try that again.

(opens the door)

HEATHER. Hiya. *(blows a bubble)*

BRIDGET. We don't want any.

HEATHER. What?

BRIDGET. You're not a friend of my grandmother's are you?

HEATHER. Not yet, Sweet Cheeks.

BRIDGET. Sorry. Uh – do you have the right – are you a…? – We didn't – How may I help you?

HEATHER. What's your name?

BRIDGET. Bridget…

HEATHER. Cool. Hey, Bridget, is this Saucy Slips, Etc?

BRIDGET. No it is not! What on earth are you talking about? What's that? *(Laughs awkwardly. Stops abruptly. Beat. Leans in, whispering.)* Why, did someone say something to you?

HEATHER. I'm looking for Sylvia Charles.

BRIDGET. Never heard of her. Well! – nice talking to you.

*(**BRIDGET** tries to shut the door. **HEATHER** stops it from closing with her high-heeled foot.)*

HEATHER. Easy, Tiger – You're gonna scuff the patent leather. I gotta talk to Sylvia – It's about a business matter.

BRIDGET. I don't think she's your type.

HEATHER. You're cute. I don't have a type. Mind if I come in?

BRIDGET. Now's not really a –

SYLVIA. *(entering from bedroom)* Who is it, Muffin Top? Oh, a guest – how nice!

HEATHER. Mind if I come in, lady?

SYLVIA. Not at all. Make yourself at home. Bridgie, is this young woman a friend of yours?

BRIDGET. Where did I put that bottle of vodka?

SYLVIA. Can I get you a drink?

HEATHER. No thank you. I never drink on the job – I take it you're - ?

BRIDGET. *(running over to* **HEATHER** *with a Bloody Mary)* Mary. Bloody Mary. With some celery. It's really good in the early afternoon…

HEATHER. No. I'm on the clock. *(blows a bubble)* And I got gum.

SYLVIA. Where do you work, Miss – *(whispering)* Bridget, what's your friend's name?

BRIDGET. Nana, I don't know who she is.

HEATHER. My name's Heather VanPree –

BRIDGET. Nana! We have things we have to do. Our deadline, remember? *(to* **SLYVIA,** *whispering)* We don't know who she is, Nana. She could be an undercover cop or something. *(to* **HEATHER.***)* We're busy.

HEATHER. I'm not staying long, Sparky! I only want to know if this very nice relative of yours is Sylvia Charles.

BRIDGET. No! Who's that?

SYLVIA. *(overlapping)* I am! This is wonderful, how on earth did you know that? – Are you here about Saucy Slips?

BRIDGET. Nana!?

SYLVIA. I'm afraid I don't really cater to young women, but Bridget that is no reason to do such a poor job welcoming her.

HEATHER. I am here about Saucy Slips, actually. But –

BRIDGET. We're closed right now. *(She hoists* **HEATHER** *up from the couch.)* Our business hours have changed. Now we're only open February 29th, so come back in four years and we'll accommodate you as best we can.

SYLVIA. Bridget, behave. Heather, how can we help you?

HEATHER. Well, I kind of like the number your assistant here is wearing – a little loose up top for ya though, huh?

BRIDGET. Funny! Why are you here?

SYLVIA. If you don't work on your customer relations, I'm demoting you to the bedroom, young lady.

HEATHER. I understand you two are busy, *(She glares at* **BRIDGET***.)* so I'll just put it all out there –

BRIDGET. *(muttering)* More?

HEATHER. I work for Saucy Lips.

SYLVIA. For whom?

HEATHER. Saucy Lips – you know, "Boldly going where no lips have gone before."

SYLVIA. Oh dear. I mean – 'Oh yes'!

HEATHER. My boss sent me down here because we got some of your boxes delivered to our company, and we figured you might have got ours.

SYLVIA. Why, this is wonderful!

BRIDGET. Yay. Wonderful! You can take your boxes and go!

SYLVIA. Great idea, Corn Bread, grab her flyers while I find the rest of Heather's things!

(**BRIDGET** *starts pulling Saucy Lips paraphernalia out from beneath the couch cushions while* **SYLVIA** *crosses to the door and tilts the coat rack. The bookshelf on the other side of the door swings open, revealing* **SYLVIA**'s *Pink collection.* **HEATHER** *watches, amazed.*)

HEATHER. Who pimped out your apartment, lady?

SYLVIA. A bootlegger.

BRIDGET. This place has a rich history of –

SYLVIA. – Revelries.

BRIDGET. –Illicit behavior. *(she runs to the front door with boxes and puts them out in the hallway)*

HEATHER. Did you design all these?

SYLVIA. Of course I did! I made them, too.

HEATHER. What about the ones in your boxes we got by mistake?

SYLVIA. My design, but a company I found did the sewing for those.

HEATHER. Your stitching here is just amazing.

SYLVIA. You sew?

HEATHER. Of course I sew! Who doesn't?

BRIDGET. I don't. *(she runs and puts more of* **HEATHER**'s *boxes in the hallway, eager for their guest to leave)*

HEATHER. Listen, Sylvia, I got to ask you – what's the deal with her?

SYLVIA. Who, Bridget? That's another one of my designs! Bridget was trying on an outfit I made for the website I'm putting together.

HEATHER. *(Lighting up immediately. Very sincerely as she blows a bubble.)* I've always wanted to be a model!

BRIDGET. If that's the case, why don't you hire her while we're here?

SYLVIA. What a good idea! She should see everything, first, though.

*(**SYLVIA** begins going around the room activating all of the tricked out gizmos in her apartment. The fireplace, closet, bookshelf and portrait hiding places are all revealed. **BRIDGET** follws behind her, closing them all.)*

BRIDGET. You didn't see anything. This was all a bad dream. *(trying to hypnotize **HEATHER**)*

HEATHER. *(ignores **BRIDGET**)* This is amazing! You run the entire store right from your apartment?

SYLVIA. I do indeed.

HEATHER. This is a much better setup than where I work. *(Chewing her bubble gum rapidly – the harder she chews, the more intensely she is thinking.)* How much do you pay your help? How much is she paying you, Sunshine?

BRIDGET. I'm getting paid in love, burnt cookies and a light prison sentence.

SYLVIA. I don't have help you see. Just Bridget who's here for the summer and –

VERA. *(grand entrance through the front door)* Parked it!

SYLVIA. …And Vera.

VERA. Who's that and where are her clothes?

SYLVIA. Vera, this is someone from Saucy Lips.

VERA. What?

BRIDGET. *(She is deaf.)* Saucy Lips. She made those flyers you liked so much. Drink?

VERA. Yes.

BRIDGET. Where did you end up parking the car?

VERA. By the clock outside the zoo entrance.

BRIDGET. The Delacorte clock? You mean you parked it on 65th?

VERA. No, I mean I parked it underneath the clock.

BRIDGET. Vera, that's *inside* Central Park.

VERA. It was on a road!

SYLVIA. That's a footpath.

VERA. Well I didn't have my glasses on! *(catches sight of* **HEATHER** *again)* Who is this, and where are her clothes?

HEATHER. Heather VanPree –

VERA. What a lovely name!

HEATHER. I work for Saucy Lips.

VERA. How remarkable. Me too! Funny we haven't met before.

HEATHER. I don't follow.

BRIDGET. She's deaf.

HEATHER. Ah.

BRIDGET. Vera! Someone is going to tow my car.

VERA. That's not the end of the world. Just be happy the owner of the Beamer I hit didn't see me –

BRIDGET and **SYLVIA.** What?

VERA. *(innocently)* What?

BRIDGET. You hit a car?

VERA. It was a love tap, kid – hardly took any paint off and I'm sure that dent can be hammered out eventually – hey, relax. Have another drink. *(loudly but meant to be conspiratorially to* **SYLVIA**, *as if* **BRIDGET** *can't hear)* Your granddaughter is very high strung.

SYLVIA. It doesn't come from my side of the family.

VERA. Of course not. How's the order coming along?

SYLVIA. OH! The order. I almost forgot.

VERA. You forgot? Haven't you done anything while I was gone?

HEATHER. Do you mean the order that got sent to us by mistake?

SYLVIA. That's the one. We've been trying to re-create it but –

VERA. It's not easy to find good help.

HEATHER. I have an idea.

BRIDGET. Great. Here we go.

HEATHER. It's really more of a business proposition.

SYLVIA. Lay it on me.

HEATHER. How about we make a trade. I'll take these boxes back to Saucy Lips, get your boxes and bring them back here –

SYLVIA. Really, you would do that?

HEATHER. Well, not for nothing. You would have to hire me. I charge a very fair hourly.

BRIDGET. Are you kidding?

HEATHER. The hourly thing was a joke. I'd want to be on payroll. Sylvia, I've always dreamed of being a model. This is a great place you set up here – I could help you run the store, provide some real customer service while you –

VERA. And me!

HEATHER. *(to* **VERA***)* –and you – design.

VERA. I'm a model, actually.

SYLVIA. What a wonderful idea!

BRIDGET. ARE YOU ALL OUT OF YOUR MINDS? *(waving the vodka bottle around as she gestures to the apartment)* This isn't a boutique!

(She begins running around to each of the hidden clothes racks, pushing buttons, pulling cords and pressing panels to get them to slide back into their hiding places.)

SYLVIA. Well it isn't a speakeasy either! Give me that bottle.

BRIDGET. No!

VERA. I wouldn't argue with her, kid.

BRIDGET. Be quiet! Enough is enough! Nana. Vera. We are having a conference immediately. *(She storms* *over to the closet and pulls out a large box, her own, and starts digging through it.)*

HEATHER. What are you doing?

BRIDGET. Getting a law book! GO AWAY.

HEATHER. No! I'm waiting here until I sign all the paperwork to start working for your Nana.

BRIDGET. FINE! Nana, get in the kitchen. Vera.

*(**VERA** doesn't hear her. She's busy chatting with **HEATHER**, curiously touching the fishnet tights.)*

Vera. VERA.

VERA. Huh? What?

BRIDGET. *(using the extremely thick, very official looking penal code textbook to point to the kitchen door)* Kitchen. Now.

*(**SYLVIA** and **VERA** exit to the kitchen, talking loudly as **BRIDGET** and **HEATHER** have a stare-down.)*

BRIDGET. Don't do anything.

HEATHER. Fine!

BRIDGET. Fine.

HEATHER. Fine!

*(**BRIDGET** exits into the kitchen. We hear the three women talking. The talking gets louder. A book slams on the table. More talking. Now yelling. Not angry yelling, mind you, the "Vera can't hear you" kind of yelling. **BRIDGET** is reading something from the book. **SYLVIA** is trying to interpret it. They are loud enough to not hear the knock on the front door. **HEATHER**, however, does. She hesitates for a minute, blowing a large gum-bubble, then shrugs and opens the door. **TOM** and **SCHMIDT** stand in the frame. **TOM** is in plain clothes now – clearly his shift has ended.)*

HEATHER. How can I help you?

SCHMIDT. Do you have any idea how much it costs to fix a BMW after a senior citizen has rammed into the side of it –?

HEATHER. Uh—?

SCHMIDT. A lot of fucking money, that's how much!

HEATHER. *(to* **TOM***)* How can I help you, handsome?

TOM. I was wondering if Bridget's home?

HEATHER. The mousey girl? She's in the kitchen. One hell of a temper on her. *(seductively)* – Why don't you stay out here where it's much more friendly?

SCHMIDT. WHERE IS SHE?

TOM. I think I'll take my chances with Bridget. Hey – uh, Mr. Schmidt?

SCHMIDT. FIX THIS!

TOM. Yeah! Okay – I'm just going to talk to them right now, okay? I'll be right back – *(He edges his way over to the kitchen door and quickly disappears inside.)*

HEATHER. *(shuts the door, blows a bubble, and eyes* **SCHMIDT***)* Bad day?

SCHMIDT. Who the hell are you?

HEATHER. Heather VanPree. Nice to meetcha. So – you know Sylvia?

SCHMIDT. *(said as if it puts a bad taste in his mouth)* I've dealt with Sylvia for years.

HEATHER. Oh you have? Here, right? At her place?

SCHMIDT. Yes. This apartment always seems to suck money out of me.

HEATHER. Don't tell me you're an unhappy customer?

SCHMIDT. What the hell is that supposed to mean? How do you know Sylvia again? You're not her granddaughter are you?

HEATHER. Oh no! I'm her business associate!

SCHMIDT. Her – what?

HEATHER. I'm new, that's probably why you don't recognize me. Listen, I know the cure for a bad day
–

SCHMIDT. I bet you do –

HEATHER. Something nice and sexy for your wife to
slip on tonight will make you feel better, don't you
think?

SCHMIDT. What?

HEATHER. When was the last time you paid us a visit?

SCHMIDT. "Us?" – This morning –

HEATHER. Well, maybe you didn't get a chance to see
everything. Her pink collection is over here – *(She
points at the bookcase, trying to remember.)* Or is it over
here? *(points to the closet)*

SCHMIDT. What the –?

*(***BRIDGET** *and* **TOM** *enter from the kitchen.)*

BRIDGET. I didn't mean to yell – you caught me at a
bad time.

TOM. So you're not mad at me?

BRIDGET. Oh, Tom, no – *(She takes his hand.)*

HEATHER. No, I'm sure it's here. *(She crosses to the coat
rack.)*

TOM. Well! That explains everything – except why
you're running around in a slip.

BRIDGET. Well, I – *(sees* **HEATHER** *and* **SCHMIDT***)* What
are you doing?

HEATHER. *(Pushes the coat rack so it tilts vertically on the
wall. The bookshelf on the other side of the front door
begins to open.)* Showing a client the goods. Relax,
Sparky.

BRIDGET. NO!

*(***BRIDGET** *sprints across to* **HEATHER** *and straightens the pegboard again. The bookshelf on the other
side of the door begins to close.)*

BRIDGET *(cont.)* There are no goods! Listen, sir, you'll have to forgive her. She's a charity case – a little – woooo – you know – bonkers.

(She guides **HEATHER** *away from the wall.)*

SCHMIDT. What the hell is going on?

HEATHER. *(shaking* **BRIDGET** *off)* Now look here – *(She tilts the coat rack.)*

BRIDGET. No please! Stop that! *(She rights the coat rack.)*

TOM. Bridget, what's going on?

(The end of every line that **BRIDGET** *and* **HEATHER** *exchange is accompanied by* **BRIDGET** *straightening and* **HEATHER** *tipping the coatrack back and forth. The bookshelf keeps creeping forward and shutting itself, unnoticed by* **TOM** *and* **SCHMIDT***, who are too distracted by the quarreling women, and then by Saucy Lips items they begin to discover in the couch.)*

BRIDGET. Nothing! Nothing. Heather is – a friend of Nana's.

HEATHER. I work for her, actually.

BRIDGET. Yeah! Yes she does! She cleans and stuff.

HEATHER. No – I am a sales associate.

BRIDGET. *(between gritted teeth)* Now is not the time to be customer friendly, *Heather.*

HEATHER. Don't tell me what to do, *Bridget.*

(And with that, **HEATHER** *gives a forceful push to the pegboard. The bookshelf on the other side of the front door swings open –* **BRIDGET** *tries and fails to stop the shelf from swinging open.)*

TOM. Bridget?

BRIDGET. Oh God. I can explain –

SCHMIDT. *(delighted)* Finally!

HEATHER. Don't mind the merchandise on the floor, that belongs to my former employer. Now if you can just direct your attention to Sylvia's racks – I'm sure you're familiar with her pricing!

SCHMIDT. Thank you God.

HEATHER. And if you don't see something in here you like, there's also our lace selection!

(**HEATHER** *crosses to the closet, opens the door and pulls the light cord.*

The fake closet panel slides to the side.)

TOM. A secret passage!?

(*The lingerie platform moves forward. The rack begins to spin.*)

TOM. Suddenly this is all making sense

BRIDGET. Tom, believe me, right now nothing should be making sense.

TOM. The whips… the slips … the chains. Your Nana is running a prostitution ring, isn't she!? (*He inspects the lingerie.*) A prostitution ring for Senior Citizens! I didn't believe it when Mr. Schmidt said something fishy was going on here – but he was right!

BRIDGET. That's Mr. Shit? (*She looks around wildly to* **MR. SCHMIDT**) Oh Schmidt!

(**VERA** *and* **SYLVIA** *enter from the kitchen, mid-argument*)

VERA. It all seemed perfectly clear to me when the kid explained it – (*She runs into* **MR. SCHMIDT**.) Code red. Code red! (*She makes submarine noises and grabs* **SYLVIA**)

SCHMIDT. (*to* **VERA**) You impaled my car with your truck.

VERA. (*to* **SCHMIDT**) It was a love tap.

SYLVIA. (*Frantic, seeing that the cat's out of the bag.*) Heather, what's going on here?

HEATHER. I was just showing this guy your stuff –

SYLVIA. Perhaps we should have communicated a little more before I left you in charge.

TOM. *(to* **SYLVIA***)* Your granddaughter is a prostitute for you, isn't she?!

BRIDGET. TOM! *(She grabs a Saucy Lips item and begins to whack* **TOM** *with it.)*

SCHMIDT. *(to* **VERA***)* You know – I'm in such a good mood, I don't even care that you totaled my car.

SYLVIA. *(to SCHMIDT)* Why are you in such a good mood?

SCHMIDT. *(to* **SYLVIA***)* Because I can finally evict you from this rent-controlled paradise of yours!

SYLVIA. Don't be absurd.

SCHMIDT. Oh – I am not being absurd. I have more than enough on you right now to not only prove that you've been breaking your lease by running a boutique in my apartment building, allowing non-residents to tramp all over the premises but – what's more – and this is the real kicker – I think I might be able to get you arrested. Tom!

TOM. *(sulking)* What?

SCHMIDT. How much jail time are we looking at for a tenant opening a store on non-commercial property?

TOM. A store?

SCHMIDT. Yeah, a store –

TOM. You mean, you aren't going to press charges about the prostitution?

SYLVIA. Tom! How dare you suggest such a thing? Now, I might run a naughty negligee line, but I would never employ *(whispers)* prostitutes.

BRIDGET/HEATHER. *(snorts/giggles)*

TOM. Oh thank God – Bridge, I'm so sorry that I –

SCHMIDT. Focus, officer! How much time are we looking at?

TOM. Oh, uh, I'm not sure – maybe –

SCHMIDT. Who cares! The point is, after years of getting off scot-free paying next to nothing and making my life a living hell, I finally – FINALLY – get to take you for every cent you're worth. I'm sure they have a very nice assisted living cell for you to wait out the rest of your days. In the meantime, I'll quadruple the rent on this place, get a rich hotshot in here, and finally make bank!

(There is a knock on the door.)

SCHMIDT. Don't interrupt me!

(HEATHER sheepishly opens the door anyway. CLAIR SCHMIDT stands in the frame. She is in her mid 60s, sophisticated and forceful. She is also married to the only other SCHMIDT in the room. She wears the pants in their relationship, but a dress skirt currently.)

SYLVIA. Oh Clair! I'm so glad you're here –

CLAIR. I'm sorry I was a few minutes late, Sylvia. Gil, what are you doing here?

SCHMIDT. I'm evicting this – you know her?

CLAIR. Of course I do. Daddy loved Sylvia. We always used to visit here together.

SYLVIA. Yes – we did have a very good landlord – tenant relationship. You could have taken a page from his book you know –

SCHMIDT. What – what the hell are *you* doing here?

CLAIR. I'm picking up my order and few other things.

SYLVIA. Oh yes, Vera, Bridget, Heather – I'd like you all to meet my oldest, dearest and best client, Clair Schmidt.

BRIDGET. She's your big client?

VERA. What? What's going on?

SYLVIA. The one and only –

BRIDGET. The landlord's *wife* is your big client? Why didn't you tell us that?

SYLVIA. It didn't seem important. Clair, dear, a bit of bad luck with your big order. It got delivered to the wrong address. I'll have to get it to you tomorrow, is that okay?

CLAIR. Yes of course, the dress rehearsal isn't until tomorrow night –

(**CLAIR** *looks around at all of the astonished faces. She and* **SYLVIA** *are the only ones who seem composed. Explaining.*)

I'm the arts director at the Happy Valley Retirement Community. I'm directing an edgy version of *The Pajama Game* and Sylvia made some of the costumes –

SCHMIDT. – Dear?

CLAIR. Yes, Gil, what is it? What on earth is going on here?

BRIDGET. Your husband was talking about how he plans to evict my grandmother and shut down her business –

CLAIR. Nonsense! *(to* **SCHMIDT***)* He won't do that.

SCHMIDT. I – I won't?

CLAIR. No. Let's think this through in a way you can most clearly understand. *(She takes him by the arm and gently guides him downstage center.)* You know that black lacey thing I bought for our anniversary last month? And that certain *something* you like taking off of me so much?

SCHMIDT. *(cannot formulate words.)*

CLAIR. …Sylvia makes those. So, if you evict her, or shut down her business – or any combination thereof, I will be wearing nothing but flannel pants and old, smelly T-shirts to bed from now on. In other words, if you shut her down, I'll shut you down.

SCHMIDT. *(cannot formulate words)*

CLAIR. What time shall I come by tomorrow, Sylvia?

HEATHER. I can run back to Saucy Lips and pick up the boxes right now, if you want!

SYLVIA. That would be perfect, Heather dear –

HEATHER. I know I messed up, but do I still have a job?

CLAIR. Of course you do, dear. Doesn't she, Gil?

SCHMIDT. *(distracted)* Uh – yes. What? Yes.

SYLVIA. Mr. Schmidt! Does this mean you're not going to shut down my business?

SCHMIDT. *(looks at his wife, who has her arms crossed and it standing at the door, waiting for him)* Not shutting you down.

BRIDGET. Or evicting her?

SCHMIDT. Not doing that either.

CLAIR. You're a lamb, Gil. *(Crosses to the door.)* Oh, and I want the dinner made and the laundry done by the time I get home. And Sylvia, I'll take five of those pointy red things in the hallway. *(She exits.)*

BRIDGET. Tom? What about you – are you going to, you know, report her?

TOM. Who, me? I'm off duty. I didn't see anything.

BRIDGET. Oh Tom! *(running-tackle hugs him, and gives him a big kiss)*

HEATHER. I'll go get the boxes.

VERA. Where are you going?

HEATHER. *(She is deaf.)* TO GET THE BOXES.

VERA. I MEANT THE ADDRESS. The hearing aid still has some juice left in her. Hey, I'll drive you! It'll be faster.

(She wheels her walker to the door, **HEATHER** *in tow, and they exit.)*

(**BRIDGET** *and* **TOM** *are still kissing.*)

SYLVIA. Thank you –

SCHMIDT. I don't want to talk about it –

SYLVIA. Okay.

SCHMIDT. Okay. (*He walks to the front door. Stops. Turns around. Resentfully.*) I just have to say – you do make some fine lingerie. Very – ahem – detailed.

SYLVIA. I appreciate the male perspective. (*beat*) I've been thinking, maybe it's time I gave you a little more money.

SCHMIDT. What do you mean?

SYLVIA. I could give you a small cut of the profits – sort of a second rent, for the store?

SCHMIDT. How much?

SYLVIA. Ten percent.

SCHMIDT. Twenty.

SYLVIA. Maybe we should ask Clair what she thinks –

SCHMIDT. Ten sounds good. We'll iron out the details later.

SYLVIA. Let's iron them out now. Shall we?

(**SYLVIA** *crosses to him and takes his arm. He shakes his head, but is smiling, and together, they exit.* **BRIDGET** *and* **TOM** *part from their kiss.*)

TOM. Bridget, I –

BRIDGET. One second, Tom. You have a little something on your face.

(*She smiles and reaches out to rub his cheek gently with one hand.*)

BRIDGET. Wow. Nana was right! Your skin *is* really soft!

(*They both laugh and he pulls her into another long, passionate kiss.*)

(*blackout*)

The End

PROPERTIES LIST

Moving boxes
"Modern" throw Pillows
Walker
Santa Mugs
Lemonade Pitcher
Lingerie in clothing bags
Other lingerie
Lots and lots of lingerie
Geriatric shoes made to look like slippers (or other types of hilarious slippers)
Two framed paintings/posters
Small note pad
Canvas bag
Camera
3 fancy (read: funny) lingerie-like outfits for Vera, Sylvia and Bridget
More boxes.
Moving Dolly
S&M paraphernalia – re: whips, chains, leather bras with pointy cups, bolts of weird and hilarious looking fabrics, wigs, fish net tights, belts with studs in them and other sundry items that will get a laugh
Flyers. Lots of flyers.
Knit blanket
Car keys
Heavy looking "Law" books

For information regarding set decoration and obtaining props from the original production of *NANA'S NAUGHTY KNICKERS*, email nanasnaughtyknickers@gmail.com

Closet Mechanism, "Nana's Naughty Knickers"

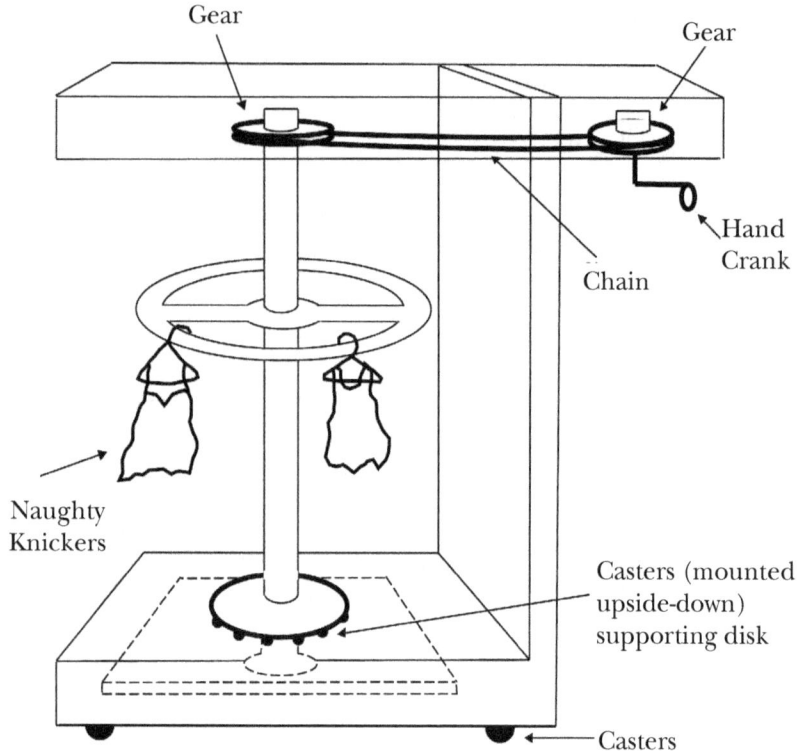

Gear

Gear

Chain

Hand Crank

Naughty Knickers

Casters (mounted upside-down) supporting disk

Casters

The entire mechanism slides forward out of the closet. A central pole supports the circular clothes rack. The pole has a gear with sprockets, connected to a second gear by chain. Bicycle parts can be used, with a number of bicycle chains strung together, or parts can be obtained at a hardware or farm supply store. The second gear is turned manually, offstage by a hand crank. The gear and chain mechanism are concealed by the ceiling of the closet. Turning these gears will rotate the clothes rack, producing the effect of endless lingerie.

Nana's Naughty Knickers
Groundplan

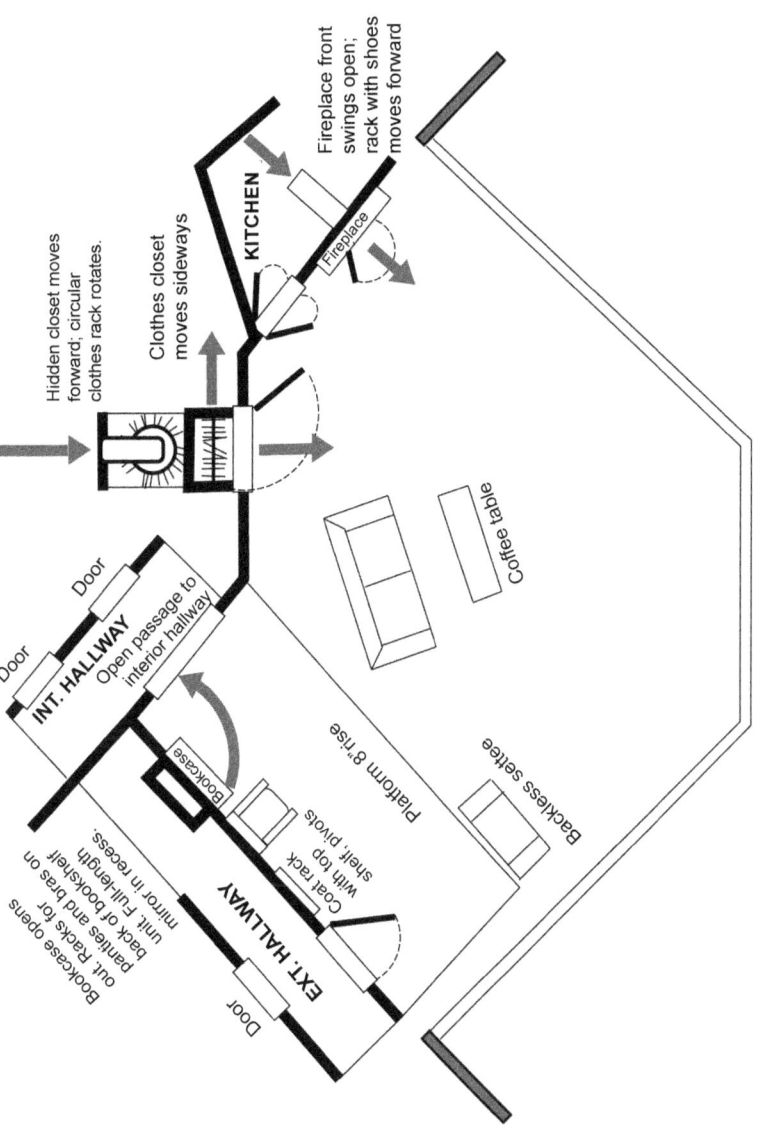

OTHER TITLES AVAILABLE FROM SAMUEL FRENCH

FLAMINGO COURT

Luigi Creatore

Comedy / 3m, 2f, with doubling (Character ages range from 60s to 89. 5 to 10 actors may be used depending on doubling or tripling roles.)

This three part "slice of life" takes place in three different condos and has audiences laughing at the truth they see in what might be their own neighbors - only zanier. *Flamingo Court* has ten characters. In the New York production, five actors played all the roles. Producers may want to follow the above pattern, or cast up to ten actors. In any case, audiences respond to this trilogy with uproarious laughter and leave feeling they have experienced great entertainment.

ANGELINA, in 104, is a Neil-Simonesque three character piece that starts with smiles and grows into a hilarious, audience-howling ending.

CLARA, in 204, is the shortest (ten to twelve minutes) piece. It deals with two characters in a poignant look at the problems of aging and separation. Powerful theater!

HARRY, in 304, a five character play - and the wackiest - deals with an eighty-nine year-old gentleman who is battling his greedy daughter at the same time that he gets involved with an aging hooker. When the daughter and the hooker meet "the audience laughs up a Florida-worthy hurricane!" (John Simon, Bloomberg News)

"Laughs galore! Without question, the funniest play in new york today! A 'must-see' theatrical event for audiences of all ages. Powerhouse performances from Anita Gillette and Jamie Farr."
– UPI

OTHER TITLES AVAILABLE FROM SAMUEL FRENCH

A NIGHT IN PROVENCE

Robin Hawdon

Comedy / 3m, 3f

From the author of *Don't Dress for Dinner*

Ah, Provence! The French Riviera. Where the well-to-do rent luxury villas for exorbitant sums in order to get their annual fix of sun, sea, and haute cuisine. However, imagine the crisis if one such sumptuous place was double booked. Worse – imagine it triple booked! By a French couple, an English couple, and heaven forbid, an Irish/American couple. Marriages have foundered on less. Add the ingredients of copious champagne, heightened sexual impulses, and ingrained cultural differences, and the European Union could well implode!

The USA and Europe have seen many comedies by Robin Hawdon, but none to threaten international relations on this scale.

"Now this admirable dinner theatre is reducing audiences to helpless laughter once more with this consistently entertaining playwright's latest work...makes for a great night out."
– *Oxford Times*

"Chaos, banter, and sexually charged jokes ensue when three couples clash at a holiday villa in Provence...This fast-paced romp was a joy to watch from start to finish...A wonderful way to spice up a chilly evening."
– *Wokingham Times*

"An overcrowded French holiday villa makes for a houseful of laughs... Robin Hawdon keeps the sexual frisson simmering in one of the Mill's unqualified successes..."
– *Reading Evening Post*

"...The audience's delight at the unpredictable final scene indicates the ultimate success of this fast moving comedy...A thoroughly enjoyable evening at the theatre."
– *Henley Standard*

SAMUELFRENCH.COM

OTHER TITLES AVAILABLE FROM SAMUEL FRENCH

NEVER KISS A NAUGHTY NANNY

Michael Parker

Farce / 4 or 5m, 2f / Interior

Mr. Broadbent, a developer and builder, has created "THE HOUSE OF THE FUTURE". He has filled it with gadgets such as: self lighting fire places, a self cleaning bathroom, central trash disposal units, automatic closets, hidden telephones, and his masterpiece "The Personal Ion Chamber". The house, however, has remained unsold for four years, probably because, as we see in the course of the play, most of the innovations of the future fail to work properly.

He has, at last found prospective buyers, Fred and Gladys McNicoll, and invites them to stay in the house. He is determined to offload this huge "White Elephant". He bribes two members of his staff, Casey Cody and Ben Adams, to pose as a married couple, who are renting the house. They are to extol its virtues and explain how everything works. He is pulling out all the stops. The fridge is full of expensive wine and he has hired a chef to prepare a gourmet meal. Unknown to The McNicolls', he even has his maintenance man Eddie Cott on hand to make running repairs. He thinks he has all the bases covered.

When Gladys hears Casey refer to Mr. Cott by name, the cat seems to be out of the bag, but Casey quickly recovers by saying she didn't say "Mister Cott" but "Mm Turcotte", the children's nanny. Eddie Cott now spends the rest of the play as Nanny Turcotte. A surprise visitor, Mr. Brooks, takes an almost insane fancy to "Nanny" who now has to defend 'her' honor, as well as fix the gadgets, all of which, without exception, misbehave.

"In this play, technology that doesn't work is just plain fun. Two hours of enjoyment and laughter."
– *The Seminole Beacon, Tampa*

"I was laughing so much I could barely hold the camera still."
– WVTV Fox 13

OTHER TITLES AVAILABLE FROM SAMUEL FRENCH

SEX PLEASE, WE'RE SIXTY

Michael Parker and Susan Parker

Farce / 2m, 4f

Mrs. Stancliffe's Rose Cottage Bed & Breakfast has been successful for many years. Her guests (nearly all women) return year after year. Her next door neighbor, the elderly, silver-tongued, Bud "Bud the Stud" Davis believes they come to spend time with him in romantic liaisons. The prim and proper Mrs. Stancliffe steadfastly denies this, but really doesn't do anything to prevent it. She reluctantly accepts the fact that "Bud the Stud" is, in fact, good for business. Her other neighbor and would-be suitor Henry Mitchell is a retired chemist who has developed a blue pill called "Venusia," after Venus the goddess of love, to increase the libido of menopausal women. The pill has not been tested. Add to the guest list three older women: Victoria Ambrose, a romance novelist whose personal life seems to be lacking in romance; Hillary Hudson, a friend of Henry's who has agreed to test the Venusia: and Charmaine Beauregard, a "Southern Belle" whose libido does not need to be increased! Bud gets his hands on some of the Venusia pills and the fun begins, as he attempts to entertain all three women! The women mix up Bud's Viagra pills with the Venusia, and we soon discover that it has a strange effect on men: it gives them all the symptoms of menopausal women, complete with hot flashes, mood swings, weeping and irritability! When the mayhem settles down, all the women find their lives moving in new and surprising directions.